THUMP

A NOVEL

AVRAHAM AZRIELI

Author photograph by Richard Dalcin

Printed in the United States by CreateSpace, Charleston, SC (Paperback Edition, 2013)

ISBN: 1494281759
ISBN 13: 9781494281755
Library of Congress Control Number: 2013921803
CreateSpace Independent Publishing Platform
North Charleston, South Carolina

ALSO BY AVRAHAM AZRIELI

Fiction:

The Masada Complex – A Novel
The Jerusalem Inception – A Novel
The Jerusalem Assassin – A Novel
Christmas for Joshua – A Novel
The Mormon Candidate – A Novel

Nonfiction:

Your Lawyer on a Short Leash
One Step Ahead – A Mother of Seven Escaping Hitler

AUTHOR'S WEBSITE:

www.AzrieliBooks.com

PART I:

Fall

CHAPTER 1

Lying on his back, Thump bench-pressed fifty-pound dumbbells while Tiffany did low-resistance bicep curls. She didn't care much for weightlifting, but a bit of muscle pain was a fair price to pay for the pleasure of watching him give his all in Spandex shorts and a sleeveless shirt, sweat shimmering on his ebony skin. He grunted through the last set, his muscles bulging. When he finally dropped the dumbbells, she clapped, and he laughed.

Next in their routine was the cardio room. It held over sixty machines, ridden hard by the early crowd of mostly young African Americans who, like Tiffany and Thump, had remained in the neighborhood after graduating from the University of Baltimore.

They ran for thirty minutes, wearing headphones connected to individual TV screens—Tiffany's tuned to ABC's *Good Morning Baltimore,* Thump's to CNBC's *Squawk Box.* The last five minutes they went all out, turning up the speed on the treadmills until they were running at full speed. Unlike weightlifting, here she easily beat him with her long legs and lithe figure. Her sneakers tapped lightly on the spinning rubber while he hard-charged with fists pumping, soles pounding, laughter bubbling up until he gave up and jumped off the machine, pulling on the safety cord that shut it off.

Tiffany used the down arrow to slow down to a stop. She got off the treadmill and scrunched her face at him. Thump gave her a touch-and-go kiss on the lips, and they jogged to the locker rooms.

Thump was out first. He stood before the mirrored wall in the reception area to adjust his tie—a rich burgundy to complement his smoke-gray suit. Tiffany emerged a moment later in her nurse's uniform and little white cap that held her hair back from her face.

"Wow!" He made her turn to the mirror to see her reflection. "Look at you!"

Tiffany checked her reflection. "What?"

"What do you mean *what?*" He laughed. "You're delicious!"

She blew air, turning away, but was clearly pleased.

"Mr. Jefferson?"

Thump turned at the sound of his name.

A young man at the reception desk held out an envelope. "The membership forms for our new Roland Park location."

Thump took the envelope while glancing at the attendant's nametag. "Thanks for remembering, Arnie."

"My pleasure. Have a great day, Mr. Jefferson."

As they headed to the door, Tiffany asked, "Roland Park?"

"A second membership is pretty cheap." He held the door for her. "We can go there on weekends, do our exercises, have lunch."

"Why?" She stepped outside. "Is it a better gym?"

"Not really. It's the same design, same equipment. But it's in Roland Park, next door to the Baltimore Country Club."

Tiffany looked up at him, waiting for an explanation.

"It's a rich neighborhood. The membership fee is nothing compared to the upside. If I pick up even a single client—"

"Oh, I see. Will you even exercise there, or just schmooze?"

"I'll work out. Definitely."

"Makes sense. Got to keep up appearances."

"You got it, baby." He took her in his arms, grinning. "We make a good team."

"We?" She put her finger on his lips. "You don't want me there. I'll ruin it for you, totally ruin it."

"Why do you say that?"

"First of all, because rich white folk think my Louisiana twang indicates that I'm stupid. And second, because I can't turn on the BS spigot like you can."

"Ouch!" He made like he was hit in the crotch, bending in pain. "You fight dirty."

"See what I mean?" Tiffany pointed at him. "You're such a drama queen!"

They laughed and kissed and held each other while an ambulance sped by, siren wailing.

He watched her hurry up the street toward Baltimore Memorial Hospital. She glanced over her shoulder and tapped her watch. He waved and ran in the opposite direction.

Half a block away, parked against the curb, was his convertible Mini—white with checkered-flag graphics and a vanity license plate that read: *Thump!*

He lowered the soft top and drove off, rap music blasting from the speakers.

CHAPTER 2

At a McDonald's drive-through, Thump picked up two cardboard trays, each with a paper cup of coffee and an egg sandwich. He gobbled his sandwich while heading down Interstate 83. Traffic moved along well for a workday morning, a thick flow of cars streaming toward the downtown skyline.

Within ten minutes he was at the corner of Charles and Lombard. The traffic light was red, and as usual, there was his regular "customer"—a homeless black man whose name and life story Thump didn't know.

"God bless," the homeless man mumbled, accepting the McDonald's tray. "Success, health, and happiness."

The light turned green, and Thump made the turn and drove up Charles Street.

Seconds later, he was startled by a roaring engine as a red Ferrari flew by him. It cut right in front of the Mini, turned sharply, and stopped perpendicularly to the sidewalk at the entry to a parking garage under an office building.

Thump stopped behind the Ferrari, whose engine revved up repeatedly as the barrier rose. The sign above the garage read: *Private – KKG Investment Management Inc.*

Following the Ferrari, Thump drove into the garage.

He pulled into an available spot among other modest cars. Leaving the top open, he collected his laptop case, got out, and straightened his suit jacket before walking across the way to where the Ferrari had parked, steps away from the door to the lobby in one of several commodious reserved spots.

The first spot, closest to the lobby door, was marked with a sign: *Reserved – Mr. Kolbe.* It was taken by a dark-blue Rolls Royce. The second spot, now taken by the red Ferrari, was marked: *Reserved – H.D. Kingman.* The third, taken by a gray Maserati Quattroporte, was marked: *Reserved – A. Goldberg.* The fourth, taken by a silver Aston Martin, was marked: *Reserved – B. Chang.* The fifth spot wasn't taken, and the sign over it read: *Reserved – TBA.* Thump's eyes lingered on it.

The Ferrari's driver's door opened, and Henrietta Kingman's shapely legs emerged, then one of her hands, dangling a pair of high-heeled stilettos.

Thump took the shoes and slipped them onto her feet. Then he took her hand and helped her out of the low-slung Ferrari. She tilted her head to avoid disrupting her carrot-colored hair, styled in a high chignon, and slowly rose to her full height, which wasn't much. Even with the heels and hairdo, she barely reached his chin.

"Mr. Jefferson." She coughed to clear the chronic hoarseness that plagued her. "You look ravishing today."

"Back at you, Miss Kingman." Thump leaned over to peck her on the cheek. Up close, her face hinted at her age with delicate wrinkles by her eyes and downward furrows from the corners of her mouth. But her green eyes sparkled with intelligence and energy.

She slipped her hand behind his head and pulled him down, her nose at his shirt collar. "And you smell good too."

At the sound of a car entering the garage, they stepped back from each other and walked to the door. Passing through from the garage to the marbled ground-floor foyer, he held the door for her, then pressed the elevator button.

"Good luck at the hearing." Kingman glanced at her watch. "You better get going."

"I'm heading there right now." The elevator doors opened, and he put his hand by the sensor to keep it open for her.

"Don't be late." She checked herself out in the gold-framed mirror before turning back to face him. "It's a nuisance case, but we can't afford to lose it."

"I'm a bit nervous, to be honest. I've never dealt with attorneys, never even been inside a courtroom before."

"Don't worry." Kingman pressed the button for her floor. "That's why we pay lawyers the big bucks. Your job is to smile at the judge and look pretty."

They shared a laugh as the elevator doors closed between them.

Thump exited the KKG building through the tall glass doors. Cars and busses rumbled by. He jogged down the sidewalk toward Lombard Street and crossed through a gap in traffic. The homeless man looked up from his McDonald's meal and watched Thump turn right on Lombard and head up toward the gray edifice that was the Edward A. Garmatz U.S. Courthouse.

CHAPTER 3

Everyone stood as Judge Clarence entered his courtroom and settled in his chair. Nominated by President Carter as the first African American to serve as a federal district court judge in Maryland, he was now gray-haired and heavy. Nevertheless, he projected a sense of earnest purpose as he shuffled the papers before him.

The court deputy announced, "*Freedom League of West Virginia v. Boulder Charitable Trust.* Case number—"

"Very well," Judge Clarence interrupted her, "Counselors, introduce yourselves."

At the defense table, a tall man with a full head of silver hair, a golfer's tan, and a light-blue suit stood up at the defense table. His mouth opened to speak, but his opponent spoke first.

"Ruth O'Connor for the plaintiff, West Virginia Freedom League." Alone at the plaintiff's table, she was about fifty, with short, salt-and-pepper hair, no makeup, and a beige suit.

"Well, well, well." Judge Clarence peered over his glasses. "If it's not our honorable colleague from the state court, Judge *Oh–Connor.*"

"Not on the bench anymore," she said. "I'm back in practice—"

"So I've heard. Indeed." His tone was cryptic, leaving the courtroom in an awkward silence.

When it was clear he wasn't going to say anything else, O'Connor said, "If it pleases the court, I'd rather be addressed by my name like any other lawyer."

"It pleases the court very much. It does." The judge puffed his cheeks and looked over to the defense table. "Mr. Davis?"

"John W. Davis for the defendant, Boulder Charitable Trust." Davis turned halfway to introduce those seated with him. "This is my associate, Erica Dropper."

Erica stood. She was young, bespectacled, and African American.

The judge smiled for the first time. "Good morning, Miss Dropper."

"Next is Mrs. Sharon Boulder," Davis continued, "chairwoman of the trust's board of trustees."

An aging Barbie Doll with big boobs and a mannequin-tight face, Sharon Boulder shook her glorious blond mane and said, "How are you, Judge?"

He nodded. "Well, thank you."

"And from KKG Investment Management," Davis said, "Senior Associate T.M. Jefferson."

Thump stood up. "Good morning, Your Honor."

The judge smiled at Thump, motioned for him to sit, and turned to O'Connor. "You may proceed, Counselor."

Under the table, Boulder's bejeweled hand rested on Thump's thigh and gave him a squeeze. He winked at her.

"I'm looking at a copy of the charter of the Boulder Charitable Trust." O'Connor held up a sheet of paper. "The charter is clear about the trust's primary goal: '*to promote freedom and democracy.*' That's the main purpose the trust was set up by the late Hank Boulder."

At the mention of her late husband, Sharon Boulder looked up at the courtroom ceiling and sighed.

"Hank Boulder," O'Connor continued, "was a native of West Virginia. He designated my client, Freedom League, as one of the first beneficiaries of the trust."

"How many other beneficiaries?" Judge Clarence asked.

"The Boulder Trust," Davis quickly answered, "has over a hundred beneficiaries."

"That's true," O'Connor continued, "but in recent years, the trust has given less and less money to Freedom League. We believe it's because KKG Investment Management exerts undue influence on the trust and charges it exorbitant fees and expenses. We therefore ask the court to issue a temporary restraining order to prevent the trust's board from renewing KKG's management contract and require an open bidding process so that other investment management firms will be considered."

Judge Clarence looked at Davis for response.

Rising slowly, Davis buttoned his suit jacket. "Your Honor, it is not my practice to utilize blunt language, but let the record be clear that West Virginia Freedom League is a group of diehard confederacy buffs—"

"Southern heritage devotees," O'Connor said.

"—who are dedicated," Davis continued, "to perpetuating a questionable historic heritage. It's worth noting that many respectable charities have received grants from the trust, and none of them joined this action." He paused, glancing at O'Connor, challenging her to dispute the statement, which she didn't.

"Not a single other charity," Davis said, "has joined this frivolous case."

O'Connor stood. "They're not aware of KKG's high fees and excessive influence."

"It's important to remember," Davis said, "that the late Hank Boulder himself chose Daniel Kolbe, chairman of KKG, to manage the trust's financial assets."

Sharon Boulder nodded and sniffled while under the table her hand traveled up the inside of Thump's thigh until her pinky nestled in the warm fold of his crotch.

"If Mr. Kolbe handles the trust," O'Connor said, turning and pointing at Thump, "then why did he send a young ah … ah … associate?"

"African American" was what she really wanted to say, everyone in the courtroom knew, implying that KKG sent a black associate, rather than its white chairman, in order to gain the judge's sympathy.

"Your Honor," Davis said, "Mr. Kolbe directs the management of the whole firm. For the purpose of this hearing, I asked KKG to send a midlevel professional who is better acquainted with day-to-day investment management services, the nuts and bolts, if you will."

O'Connor snorted in disgust. "The nuts and bolts at KKG are made of gold. It's an uppity firm that serves only the very wealthy, and now its snobbery has infected the trust's decision-making process."

"That's an undeserved insult," Davis said. "KKG is one of Maryland's top investment management firms. Its hundred-plus employees serve many high-net-worth individuals and multigenerational family trusts, as well as arts and cultural charities—"

Judge Clarence stopped him with his hand. "I'm familiar with KKG's excellent reputation. But are the fees too high, especially in the context of a charitable trust?"

Dropper handed Davis a packet of documents.

"These exhibits," Davis said, "are copies of three academic studies by top research universities. They provide detailed analyses of leading investment management firms and their fee structure, proving that KKG's fees are industry standard, calculated as percentage of assets under management, plus customary performance bonuses."

"KKG is abusing the trust," O'Connor said. "For example, in addition to nearly seventeen million dollars in fees last year, KKG charged the trust almost two thousand dollars for a dinner."

The judge sat back in his chair. "A dinner?"

"Yes," O'Connor said. "Three senior KKG partners had dinner at Pratt Steak House, including several pricey bottles of wine, and submitted the bill to the trust." She glanced at her notes. "Nineteen hundred and thirty-four dollars."

Thump whispered to Davis, "They discussed strategy."

"Your Honor," Davis said, "it's customary to charge clients for dinner meetings when investment strategy is discussed for the sole benefit of the client."

Judge Clarence made a face. "I discuss case strategy with my law clerks over lunch every day. It never occurred to me to submit the cost of my tuna sandwich as a business expense."

Thump whispered again in Davis's ear, "We'll give them a refund and not do it again."

"As a courtesy," Davis said, "without admitting any wrongdoing, KKG agrees to refund this particular expense and will no longer charge the trust for meals."

"This sounds reasonable," Judge Clarence said. "Is Mrs. Boulder satisfied?"

Davis turned to Sharon Boulder, who smiled and nodded.

"Yes," Davis said. "She is satisfied."

O'Connor dropped her papers on the table. "We believe KKG discourages charitable distributions because its fees are based on the remaining assets!"

"Pure speculation," Davis said. "My opponent does not understand the way charitable trusts and their advisors work. Trustees decide about grants and beneficiaries, not the external investment management firm."

"I understand," O'Connor said, "how greed legitimizes this kind of financial rape—"

"That would be enough!" Judge Clarence motioned for both lawyers to sit down. "The motion is denied. Plaintiff can address its concerns about KKG directly to the board of trustees at the annual meeting next Friday, a week from tomorrow. Good day, Counselors."

Everyone stood as the judge left the courtroom.

O'Connor gathered her papers into a brown folder and turned to leave. Davis stepped forward and offered his hand, which she shook without smiling.

"Win some, lose some," Davis said.

"Apparently," she said.

"It's a pleasure having you back with us on this side of the bench."

"The pleasure is all yours."

"Touché." Davis chuckled. "How is Jerald?"

"Limping along. Thanks for remembering."

Thump joined them, offering his hand to O'Connor. She pretended not to see him and headed down the aisle and out the door.

Davis patted Thump's shoulder. "Don't take it personally, kid. When she still wore the robe over at the state court, lawyers nicknamed her Judge Rob—for *Racist Old Bitch.*"

CHAPTER 4

Descending the front steps of the courthouse, Sharon Boulder clasped Thump's arm. Below them, at the curb, her chauffeur was holding open the limousine door.

"Let's go," Boulder said. "A little ride. To celebrate."

Thump pointed up the street. "I should go back to the office—"

"You're such a smart cookie." She leaned on his arm, taking each step carefully with her high heels. "That idea, to refund the damn lunch money—you practically rescued poor John."

"That's too generous. Mr. Davis would have managed fine without me."

"No, no, you were very clever. I was impressed."

"Thank you."

"No, thank you! I will let Henrietta know what a big help you were." She patted his hand. "And a real pleasure to have around, as always."

They reached the curb. He helped Sharon Boulder into the limo and climbed in after her.

The chauffeur, Ricardo, drove slowly. Sharon Boulder and Thump lounged in the rear. Above them, the sunroof was open to the blue sky. She poured drinks, gave him one, and toasted: "To handsome men who know what has to be done!"

They clinked glasses and drank.

Ricardo arrived at an isolated spot near Fort McHenry, where he parked the limo at the water's edge and stepped out.

She giggled like a little girl, throwing back her big hair, reached over, and unbuckled his belt. Thump fished a Bull-M condom from his pocket, brought it to his teeth, and tore the wrapper.

"Ooh, the sound of a fresh condom in the morning!" She mounted him, straddling his lap. "I love it!"

CHAPTER 5

Thump stepped out of Sharon Boulder's limo in front of the KKG building. He paused before the glass doors, adjusted his pants, buttoned his jacket, and entered.

He took the elevator up to the fifth floor, used his keycard to enter, and walked down the wood-paneled hallway.

Arthur Goldberg stepped out of his office. "Great job at court today!" He was a senior partner, chubby and bald with thick glasses that made his eyes look watery. He counted some of Baltimore's richest families among his clients.

"News travels fast," Thump said.

"Davis reported that you saved the day."

"I don't know about that. Mr. Kolbe might be upset that I gave them a refund."

"Upset?" Goldberg laughed. "Two thousand dollars refund for a bunch of millions in fees? Do it any day!"

Pumping his fist in the air, Thump headed down the hallway.

He poked his head into an office marked *Human Resource Manager.* "Good morning!"

Tecumseh Tekatawa turned in her chair. She was a voluptuous woman with classic Native American features and very long, straight hair. "And an exceptionally good morning for you, from what I've heard."

He laughed. "Maybe I should have gone to law school."

"It's never too late."

"Oh no, not me. No more school. Listen, where do we stand with that raise I recommended for Andy?"

"No can do," she said. "Your assistant is not eligible until next year."

"How can we make him eligible?"

"I don't make the rules."

"Bend the rules," Thump said. "It'll set you free."

"Free and unemployed."

Thump laughed. "Nah, KKG jobs are for life."

Thump placed the laptop on his desk between the two framed photos. One showed him with Tiffany on a sunny Florida beach, the other with his mother at his college graduation eight years earlier. His office was tight, but its large window brought in light and a partial view of Camden Yards.

His assistant, Andy, followed him into the office. He was skinny and bleached blond, and his voice had an effeminate intonation. "Rumor's going around that KKG was rescued today by—"

"By the judge," Thump said.

"He liked you, didn't he?"

"Like a bro from da hood. Any messages?"

Thump hung his jacket while Andy used the phone on the desk to dial voicemail. The system announced, "*You have one message … from … Henrietta Kingman.*"

"Hi. It's me." Her distinct voice, hoarse and scratchy, was immediately recognizable. "I'm down in Annapolis to pitch our services to the Teachers' Pension Fund. Congrats on thumping those West Virginia pests at court—great job!" She cleared her throat. "Listen, I just heard back from a woman I met at a gallery opening last night. Kitty Loutton. Husband died recently and left a food business, which is being sold by the estate for about twelve million, which means she'll need investment managers. Bottom line is, she's a hot prospect. I want to sign her up while our competitors are still in foreplay. She'll call you today. Take good care of her. I want her hooked quick."

Andy hit the speaker button, ending the call. "Loutton already called. What do you want me to do?"

"Call her back. Set it up."

The expression on Andy's face was a mix of doubt and repulsion.

"Don't get all Mother Teresa on me." Thump sat down and turned on his laptop. "Twelve million in assets would generate annual management fees of two to three hundred thousand dollars for the firm."

A single shrug of one shoulder was Andy's only response.

"Are you even listening?" Thump glared at him. "Three hundred thousand dollars every year! Again and again! Year in and year out for ten, twenty, even thirty years—do the math!"

"Three, six, even nine million dollars."

"Exactly! So what's a little personal inconvenience for me, doing what it takes, if it means signing up this size of an account? It'll take a herd of small clients to generate that kind of money—forty or fifty doctors and lawyers and drycleaners, OK?"

"OK. You're the boss."

"You bet I am!"

"Are we dropping the hunt for little guys?"

"Not at all. Got to remember hedging the risks. Can't have all our eggs in Miss Kingman's basket, right?"

"Right."

"Any interesting finds on the EMT online records site?"

"Actually, there is something. Give me a second."

Andy ran out to his cubicle and came back with his note pad.

"Last night," he said, "there was an interesting event. It's a nine-one-one call from a home in The Orchards neighborhood. Male, about sixty-five, was unresponsive. EMTs got there, performed CPR. He was declared dead at the scene. Likely cause was cardiac arrest."

"So far so good," Thump said. "What did you find out?"

Andy flipped through his notes. "Googled the address. The home is owned by Elizabeth and Stanley Davenport. His name came up as part owner of an HVAC service and repair business called Mid-Atlantic Comfort Indoors. I called this morning. Message says they're closed due to a loss in the family."

"Blue-collar folks with some money. They need us the most. Anything else comes up about the deceased?"

"Nothing yet. Not even funeral arrangements."

"Good. I'll be the first in the door—if they let me in."

Andy handed him a sheet of paper. “Here’s the address and information.”

Thump looked at it. “I’ll go there tonight. Go buy a nice bouquet, will you?”

CHAPTER 6

Thump peered at the list on his laptop screen and punched in a telephone number. A woman answered. "BC Medical Center, Urology Department. Can I help you?"

"Dr. Bernholz please," Thump said. "This is a personal matter."

"Hold please."

A few minutes later, a man's voice came on the line. "This is Dr. Bernholz."

"T.M. Jefferson here," Thump said. "KKG Investments. We specialize in assisting physicians—"

"Not interested."

"Are you a baseball fan? We're hosting a pregame party—"

The line went dead.

Thump blew air through pursed lips, glanced at the list, and dialed again.

Two hours and a dozen dead-end calls later, Thump was eating a chicken salad from a Styrofoam box when another doctor came on the line.

"This is Dr. Greenbaum at gastroenterology. Who's this?"

"T.M. Jefferson, KKG Investments. May I have a moment of your time?"

"What is this about?"

"I recently did an analysis of a pharmaceutical company's stocks—"

"I don't have time to talk right now."

"We could discuss it over a gastronomical experience at Giullianno's. Our firm maintains an account there, and I'd be happy to—"

The doctor hung up.

Thump threw the Styrofoam in the trash basket, stretched for a moment, and made the next call.

"Dr. Mendelssohn, otolaryngology."

"Good afternoon, Doctor. T.M. Jefferson, KKG Investments—"

"Are you a patient of mine?"

"Not yet," Thump said, "but I'll listen to your sales pitch if you listen to mine."

Dr. Mendelssohn laughed.

Thump typed quickly, pulling up the website for the Baltimore Symphony. "Dr. Mendelssohn, our private booth at the Baltimore symphony hall—"

"You'll be wasting your time. I'm a mutual funds kind of a guy."

Thump peered at the laptop screen. "Here we go: next Sunday they're playing Felix Mendelssohn's 'Overture.' Surely you'd like to attend, Dr. Mendelssohn?"

"You're persistent, I'll give you that."

"Free food and drinks, Mendelssohn family music, and we'll have a little time to talk business. What do you say?"

"Fine. Send me two tickets. My wife will be happy."

The call ended, and Thump yelled, "Yes!"

He slapped the desk, causing Tiffany's photo to fall. He picked it up, kissed it, and propped it back in place.

Eight calls later, he got lucky again at the department of sports medicine.

"Good afternoon, Dr. Jonas. Do you enjoy boating?"

After a brief hesitation, the doctor said, "I do. Who is this?"

"T.M. Jefferson, KKG Investment Management Inc. Our firm's yacht, the *Steady Hands*, is docked at the Inner Harbor. Perhaps you've seen it?"

"Yes, I think so. It's one of the biggies, isn't it? White and gold?"

"That's the one! Please let me take you out for a spin, catch some fish, talk investments?"

"Maybe. Send me a letter, OK? Good-bye."

He hung up.

Thump yelled, "Andy!"

The assistant poked his head in the door.

"Dr. Jonas from BC Medical, sports medicine. He'll go fishing with me on *Steady Hands*. Find out when the yacht is available, send him a letter with possible dates, and follow up until he commits."

Andy saluted and left.

CHAPTER 7

From his office window Arthur Goldberg noticed a silver Bentley coupe pull to the curb below. Not a minute later, Thump exited the building and approached it. A woman stepped out of the driver's seat. She wore a loose cotton dress over a generous figure. Her wrists were laden with gold bracelets, and her shoulder-length hair was dyed deep brown.

They shook hands, and Thump held the door as she got back behind the wheel. He walked around the Bentley and got in on the passenger side. A moment later, the car sailed away, out of sight.

Goldberg checked his watch. It was three in the afternoon. He picked up his phone and called Thump's office.

"Mr. Jefferson's office," Andy answered.

"Arthur Goldberg here. May I speak with him?"

"I'm sorry, Mr. Goldberg. He's not here right now. Would you like his voicemail?"

"No need." Goldberg glanced at the street below. "I'll call his mobile."

There was a long pause before Andy said, "He's in a meeting with a potential client. If it's urgent, maybe I can help?"

"No, that's fine. Client development is our first priority. I'll catch him later."

Driving down a two-lane country road with large mansions visible through the trees, Mrs. Loutton glanced at Thump with a nervous smile. He smiled back and loosened his tie. "You know," he said, "if you shift manually, the motor helps you slow down ahead of a curve, or speed up."

"Really? I never try anything like that. I'm a very boring driver."

"Here, let me show you." Thump took her right hand from the steering wheel to the gearshift. His large, black hand rested on her feminine white hand. Together they moved the gearshift knob sideways to manual mode and then downward. The car slowed down as it downshifted.

"Now," he said, "press harder on the gas."

She did, and as the Bentley accelerated hard, she yelped, then laughed.

"Feels good," he said, "doesn't it?"

"Yes!" A curve was coming up, and she turned the wheel sharply. "Oops!"

The right tires left the asphalt and dropped onto the dirt shoulder. Thump reached over with one hand, grabbed the steering wheel, and corrected expertly.

"You're doing great," he said. "Gun it again!"

She did, and the car roared forward.

He clapped. "Excellent!"

Farther down the road she slowed down and pointed. "That's my street, over there on the hill."

Thump looked at the view. "That's a gorgeous area. How long have you lived here?"

"Quite a while. It's a wonderful house, though a bit too big now that I live alone." She hesitated. "We can stop by, get something to drink."

"Would you like to do that?"

She blushed. "Why not?"

CHAPTER 8

Thump parked his Mini in front of a house that was illuminated with soft landscape lighting. It was a split-level, at least forty or fifty years old, but greatly improved. The owners had added a sunroom on one side and a deck on the other end, as well as a front portico with a pitched roof and stone columns.

He verified the address, collected the flowers from the passenger seat, and walked up to the front door.

The name, etched in a brass plaque, was *Davenport.* A black ribbon was threaded over it.

He rang the bell.

The door was opened by a white man, about thirty, muscular and bearded, wearing jeans and a T-shirt that said *MID-ATLANTIC COMFORT INDOORS.*

Thump handed him the bouquet of flowers. "Our deepest condolences."

"Thanks." He took the bouquet, reached into his pocket and pulled out a dollar bill. "Here you go."

"Oh no, the flowers are from us." Thump smiled and offered his card. "T.M. Jefferson. KKG Investment Management. We received notice of your unfortunate loss and wanted to offer our help as soon as possible."

He looked at the card. "What's this about?"

"We're investment advisors, been in business over forty years. It's our mission to advise families in financial transitions, help secure their future. Perhaps your mother is available for a few minutes?"

"We'll call you." He shut the door before Thump could say anything more.

Through the open windows, a woman's voice could be heard. "Junior? Who's at the door?"

"Nobody, Mom," Junior yelled back. "Some black guy selling shit."

CHAPTER 9

The next morning, at the corner of Lombard and Charles Street, Thump stopped to deliver the usual McDonald's tray with coffee and a sandwich to the homeless man, who in return delivered his blessing: "Health, success, and happiness."

Ten minutes later, Thump was at his desk, sipping the last of his coffee while making his first cold call of the day.

"Dr. Le Pierre, plastic surgery." The man spoke with a French accent.

"Hello!" Thump tossed the cup into the waste basket, leaped from his chair, and through the open door beckoned Andy. "Good morning, Doctor!"

"Who is this?"

"T.M. Jefferson here. How are you?"

"Very well. Your name is not familiar. Are you a patient?"

"Truth is, I'm not a patient." Thump turned to Andy and whispered in his ear, "Best French restaurant?" Then, back to the phone loudly, he said, "I'm an investment advisor with KKG Investment Management Inc. Are you familiar with our firm?"

"This is not a good time—"

Andy grabbed a paper and a pen and scribbled quickly.

"I know," Thump said, "I was wrong to disturb you at work, and as my penance, I'll be taking you to dinner at—" He grabbed Andy's note and read from it. "Chez François!"

As they waited for a response, Andy held up crossed fingers.

"Chez François is, ah, a very expensive restaurant—"

"My treat," Thump said. "And I promise that my sales pitch won't last beyond the—how do you call?—*L'apéritif*!"

Andy made an expression of being impressed.

"Besides," Thump added, "as a courtesy to you, I can refer some patients, well-to-do ladies who could definitely use your services. What do you say?"

"It is difficult," Dr. Le Pierre said. "My calendar is very busy."

"Doesn't matter. Any evening you're free, I'll make myself available."

"OK, OK. Call me next week. We set a date, OK?"

"Perfect! Talk to you next week then!"

"OK. Good-bye."

"Au revoir!" Thump hung up and gave Andy a high five.

Laughter came from the door. They turned to see who it was, finding Goldberg with Bo Chang, a young partner, who asked, "Are we invading France?"

"It's the other way," Thump said. "We're trying to have France invade us."

"Better go there," Chang said. "I went to Paris last July—what a place!"

"I'd like to see Paris before I die," Thump said.

"You'll get there one day," Goldberg said. "But in the meantime, Mr. Kolbe wants to see you in his office."

The two partners left. Thump started after them but paused as Andy grabbed his jacket off the hook and helped him put it on.

CHAPTER 10

Mr. Kolbe's corner office was huge. It was furnished with wood and leather, and the Persian rugs seemed too expensive to step on. Thump entered behind Chang and Goldberg.

"Here's the man." Daniel S. Kolbe, chairman of KKG Investments, got up and circled his vast desk, his hand extended. "Excellent result yesterday with that pesky little charity."

"Freedom League of West Virginia." Thump shook his hand, which was as large and firm as his.

"Where they belong!" Mr. Kolbe buttoned his suit jacket and tugged on the lapels to smooth out any creases. At seventy, the firm's founder was tall and muscular, with a tanned face, swept-back snowy hair, and the youthful gait of a golf player who shunned the carts in favor of walking the eighteen holes, carrying his gear and winning every round, unless business considerations required letting someone else win.

Henrietta Kingman rose from an armchair and made Thump bend lower so that she could kiss the air by his cheek. She wore a turquoise silk skirt and blouse, which accentuated the delicateness of her slim body. Her hair appeared freshly dyed in a lively carrot shade and piled in the usual high chignon. At fifty-six, she exuded confidence, as well as the toughness of a woman who had managed to reach the top in a male-dominated business.

She held on to him and said hoarsely, "You really thumped them!"

"And saved our biggest contract," Chang said.

“Indeed.” Mr. Kolbe poured wine into glasses, handed them out, and toasted, “To our rising star!”

Everyone raised glasses and drank.

“Not to spoil a party,” Goldberg said, “but it could be a pyrrhic victory. The trust’s board of trustees might scrutinize us, question our fees, our strategy—”

“Arthur,” Kingman said, “you’re such a pessimist.”

Mr. Kolbe sat down, wineglass in hand. “My friend Hank Boulder, before he died, asked me to take good care of his charitable trust, to manage it wisely so its assets would continue to grow rather than fizzle out like so many other charitable trusts. You all should understand that, for me, this isn’t only about our fees. It’s an ethical, moral duty to continue the work entrusted to our firm by a great businessman and dear friend.”

“Of course.” Kingman sat on the sofa’s armrest beside Mr. Kolbe, who glanced up at her. She checked her hair. “It’s truly outrageous for anyone to question our commitment to the trust and its success.”

Everyone nodded in agreement and sipped wine.

“Anyway,” Kingman continued, “I think we’re safe now. I spoke with Sharon Boulder last night. As board chairwoman, she’ll make sure the trustees vote to renew our contract. All we need to do is keep a low profile and keep her happy.” As she said it, Kingman smiled at Thump, who smiled back.

Mr. Kolbe saw the exchange of smiles. He emptied his glass and said to Thump, “What do you think?”

Thump took a long moment to consider.

“I know what he’ll say,” Chang said. “Give them another refund!”

Everyone laughed.

“Sharon Boulder,” Thump said, “is on our side. That’s true. She runs the board and she’ll use her influence to advocate for us so that the board extends the KKG management agreement by another year. But what if these guys from West Virginia keep making trouble? What if our role becomes a contentious issue, or the value of our services is questioned in view of our substantial fees. I mean, if it comes to a real confrontation, then Sharon

Boulder's support might be insufficient. She only has one vote, and trustees are notoriously fickle."

"Another pessimist?" Kingman, arms folded on her chest, shook her head. "There's no risk of Sharon losing control."

"Risk always exists," Goldberg said. "It's inherent to the human condition."

"Especially in business," Mr. Kolbe said. "Our whole existence as a firm is founded on helping people manage risk. Please continue, Mr. Jefferson."

"We could keep a low profile." Thump walked across the room, taking charge. "Hide behind Sharon Boulder and play it safe. Or we can be proactive. We can take a lead on how the Boulder Trust uses its funds and how it meets its charitable and social goals."

"No way," Kingman said. "We're the investment manager. We can't interfere with grants."

"That's correct," Goldberg said. "The beneficiaries are already upset with KKG's influence. Invading nonbusiness aspects of the trust is an invitation to controversy."

"Not only that," Chang said. "Our expertise is selecting companies to invest in. We're hired to increase value and maintain financial strength, not dispense charity. How are we supposed to help the trust with its goals? Are we going to suggest distributions? Give grants to charities we like?"

"That," Goldberg said, "would be an outright violation of the—"

"Hold on!" Thump held up his hands. "Who said anything about grants or distributions? Let them distribute the minimum required by the IRS to qualified charities. But beyond that, we can offer great value."

They watched him, waiting.

"My idea is this: We'll propose to the Boulder Trust's board a new strategic plan, an investment program that mirrors the trust's social goals by investing in socially responsible companies. The trust will make money and satisfy its goals simultaneously." Thump paused to let his words sink in. "Instead of giving away more good money to poorly run charities, the trust can have its cake and eat it too."

Everyone looked at Mr. Kolbe, waiting to see how he would respond.

Mr. Kolbe started clapping. “Mr. Jefferson,” he said, “you’re a devious man of integrity!”

They all burst out laughing, as if a pressure valve had opened.

“You nailed it, you really did.” Mr. Kolbe rose from the sofa. “Which makes this an opportune time to inform you that, earlier this morning, the management committee decided to promote you to vice president. Congratulations!”

Thump shook hands with Mr. Kolbe and the others. “Thank you,” he said through a fog of shock and excitement. “Thank you so much!”

“Get cracking on that strategic plan,” Mr. Kolbe said as he led him to the door. “Boulder Trust is not only our biggest client, it’s our most visible one. If the trustees go for this new strategy, the news will travel throughout the business community and help us market our services to other large trusts and pension funds.”

Thump faced him at the door. “I’ll start right away.”

“You’d better. It’s only a week until the board meeting.”

“Sir,” Thump said heartily, “I won’t disappoint you!”

“Very good.” Mr. Kolbe slapped Thump’s shoulder. “We’re counting on you.”

“Don’t worry, Dan,” Kingman said. “I’ll stay on top of him.”

Mr. Kolbe glanced at her as if he wanted to say something, but turned and went back to his desk.

Walking down the hallway with Thump, Kingman said, “Once the trustees adopt your plan, I’ll make sure to push for you to work with the trust to help implement it.”

CHAPTER 11

Everything in Kingman's office was white—the rugs, chairs, sofa, desk, even the door, padded in white leather. Kingman locked it behind them.

"Now that I think about it," she said while following him across the room, "I'm starting to wonder about your idea. Companies that promote freedom and democracy?"

Thump laughed. "Are you proud of me?"

"My pride is burning hot and wet." Kingman unhooked the top button of her blouse.

"I'm kind of proud of myself." Thump rubbed his hands. "And my presentation to the board will be an absolute killer. Knock their socks off!"

"Poof!" She pantomimed something flying away.

"I mean it. This is my chance to enter the big league!" He paused. "With your help, of course. I wouldn't even be in the room if not for you."

"We're a team, big boy." Standing before him, she looked up. "Question is, are you ready to be rich?"

"Been waiting all my life."

"Good." Kingman patted his cheek. "Kitty Loutton called, full of breathless praise for you. She promised to hire us to manage her investments."

"Bingo!"

Kingman's hand descended to his crotch. "All thanks to this."

"Customer service is the investment advisor's top responsibility."

"I trained you well." She took a deep breath. "Let's play customer and investment advisor."

"Now?" He glanced at the door. "I'm eager to start on the strategy presentation."

"Of course." She rested her hands on his shoulders, pressing down. "It'll be quick."

He went down on his knees.

"There you go." Kingman lifted her skirt.

He pulled down her panties and kissed her gently, then again.

"That's my boy." Holding on to his head, she put one leg up on his shoulder, giving him better access. "There, that's better."

He placed his hands on her buttocks, supporting her. Gradually his tongue work intensified.

Kingman gazed at the opposite wall. Her breath quickened, and waves of tremors passed through her.

When she was about to scream, Kingman pushed his head away, panting as she struggled to control herself.

Thump reached into his pocket, fished out a Bull-M condom, and tore the wrapper with his teeth. The sound of tearing made her tremble once more. She descended, facing him, and locked her hands behind his neck. Their faces were close, eyes connected, while he slipped on the condom.

She slowly descended, pinning herself on him until he filled her. Then she started moving up and down. Her eyes left his and wandered to the wall, landing on a framed photo of her with Mr. Kolbe, both of them a decade younger, in summer whites, smiling at the camera from the helm of the *Steady Hands.*

CHAPTER 12

Thump entered the office kitchenette and found Goldberg and Chang sitting at a small round table, sipping coffee and talking quietly while a wall-mounted TV reported the current numbers on Wall Street.

Goldberg saw him first. "Aha! Mr. Vice President!"

"Where?" Thump looked over his shoulder.

Chang laughed.

Opening the fridge, Thump said, "I'll have to get used to it."

"The title is nothing," Goldberg said. "Wait till you see your next paycheck."

"Now you're talking!" Thump took a water bottle from the fridge. "How much is the raise?"

"Fifty percent," Chang said. "Do the math."

Thump looked at Goldberg for confirmation.

Goldberg nodded. "VP is an executive position, a major milestone."

"That's right," Chang said. "What are you going to spend it on?"

"I can tell you," Goldberg said. "He'll rent a nicer apartment and lease a cooler car."

"Probably. But that's not all."

"Oh!" Chang whistled. "Tell us!"

Thump took a long swig from the bottle.

"What's that?" Goldberg pointed. "There, on your pants?"

Checking himself, Thump saw a moist stain near his zipper. He grabbed a napkin and rubbed it. "Damn. It's mayo from my breakfast sandwich."

Chang bent forward, looking closely. "Looks like it came from inside."

"It does," Goldberg said. "What have you got in there? A magic geyser?"

Jogging down the hallway toward the restroom, he was chased by their laughter.

Back at his desk, Thump called Tiffany on his mobile phone. Her photo appeared on the screen, in her nurse's uniform, smiling.

"Hi! Is everything OK?"

"Sure," Thump said. "Everything's cool. I know you can't talk right now, but I also know that you'd want to hear the news as soon as possible."

"What news?"

"They made me VP."

"Oh my God! I'm so happy for you!"

"For us."

Tiffany was quiet for a moment. "For us," she repeated. "I like that."

"Good."

"Vice president," she said. "It sounds so important."

"Isn't it?" He laughed. "I can't believe they actually gave it to me. An executive position!"

"You've worked very hard for it."

"That's an understatement." He sighed. "You don't know the half of it. But from now on, it's a different story. I can be my own person."

"Have you told your mom?"

"Not yet. She's on duty. You know how they are at L and D."

"I'll go find her," Tiffany said. "She'll be so happy."

"What are you doing tonight?"

"No plans. I get off at six."

"Perfect," Thump said. "I'll pick you up from your place at seven. We'll go to Fells Point. Be hungry, OK?"

At Baltimore Memorial Hospital, Tiffany hurried down the hallway, then another, and then through doors marked *Labor & Delivery*. She peeked into rooms where women were lying in various stages of labor, some in pain, some not, some already holding babies. Finally she spotted Mrs. Jefferson in one of the rooms, making a bed for the next patient. She wore light-blue scrubs and a plastic cap on her hair.

"Here you are," Tiffany said, startling her. "I was looking for you."

"What's wrong, honey?"

"Nothing is wrong. I have some news for you."

"News? I don't like the sound of it."

"What's wrong with news?"

"It depends." Mrs. Jefferson glanced at her midsection. "You're not with a baby, are you?"

"No, I'm not pregnant." Tiffany laughed. "Not even close."

"Then what?"

"They promoted him to vice president!"

Mrs. Jefferson looked upward and whispered a brief prayer of thanks. "Vice President Thurgood Marshall Jefferson," she said in wonder. "Praise the Lord!"

"Amen." Tiffany clapped. "He's taking me to dinner tonight."

Mrs. Jefferson sighed. "You better be ready with an answer."

"An answer? What's the question?"

"The question a man asks on his knees, honey. That question."

"No way." Tiffany gestured in dismissal. "We're just celebrating his promotion. That's all."

"Yeah, yeah, yeah."

"What? Did he tell you?"

"I need no telling. He's my son. I know him."

Tiffany looked at her sideways, eyes squinting.

"That's it. The way he looks at you."

"What way?"

"The blind way." Mrs. Jefferson patted Tiffany's cheek. "My son is in love with you. And who could blame him? You're a doll, beautiful, inside and out."

"Thank you." Tiffany looked down, embarrassed. "You think he will propose? Really?"

"Oh yeah. Now that he's made it in the firm, he's going to pop the question, no doubt about it."

"Then I'll say yes!"

"No, you won't." Mrs. Jefferson got up, walked to the door, and glanced outside to make sure no one was within earshot. "When a man in love proposes marriage, it's the woman's opportunity to set rules."

"Rules? Like what?"

Mrs. Jefferson patted her cheek again. "Honey, don't be naive."

"What do you mean? I shouldn't trust him?"

"Don't get me wrong. I introduced the two of you because I knew you're right for him and he's right for you. You'll be a good wife and he'll be a good husband, a good provider. You both want a good life and you're working your butts off to make it happen. But if you don't put down clear rules—"

"What are you saying?" Tiffany sat on the edge of the hospital bed. "Is he going to hurt me?"

"Not intentionally. He has a good heart, my son. He does. But he grew up without a father, you know? Like so many of our boys, he had no good role model growing up."

"He had you."

"Oh yeah, he had me to whip him into shape when he needed it. He had his mamma." Mrs. Jefferson chuckled at the memory. "But now he's a grown man, honey. He's a man, and they're all the same."

"The same what?"

"Kay. Nine."

Tiffany shook her head. "I don't know what it means."

"Dogs, honey. Men are dogs."

"Mrs. Jefferson!"

"Look around you." Mrs. Jefferson gestured. "The girls on this floor? Most of them have no husbands by their side. Do you want to lie here one day, crying alone?"

Tiffany shook her head.

"OK then. Will you listen to a woman who learned a thing or two in life?"

"Yes."

"Men are like dogs. They are needy. You know what I mean? They need lots of feeding, petting, and screwing."

Tiffany smiled, covering her mouth.

"So you give your man plenty, and you think you're safe, right? Wrong! Just like a dog, your man, who loves you dearly, will still run off after a stranger in heat—even if he's just climbed off your hot and tired body five minutes ago."

Tiffany started to protest, but Mrs. Jefferson wasn't done.

"It's their nature. So before you accept his proposal, make him swear, on his life: no going off with no strangers!"

CHAPTER 13

An early fall breeze swept in from the Chesapeake Bay and cleared the muggy evening air. Thump and Tiffany were sitting at a table in the outdoor patio of the restaurant, sharing a pile of Maryland crabs, a giant bowl of spaghetti bolognese, and a bottle of Mount Airy Pinot Grigio.

"Investment management firms," Thump was saying, "are all about Assets Under Management. That's the measuring rod for a firm's size and success. It's also how everyone looks at you individually. It's like a personal score, you know? Everyone wants to know what's your total Assets Under Management, what's the total value of all the bonds and stocks in your clients' accounts, OK?"

Tiffany nodded. "I get it."

"That's the thing. I've been working like crazy to find my own clients, build my own base, earn my place as equal, you know? But now, this opportunity, it could be a shortcut."

"How?"

"Because at KKG, even though there are lots of clients, the Boulder Trust is huge. It's almost twenty percent of the firm's total Assets Under Management. Originally Mr. Kolbe was managing it personally, but later he brought Kingman in to co-manage the account with him. Now, if they bring me in also, do you realize what it would mean?"

"Aha."

"It'll mean partnership! A huge salary, profit sharing, unlimited expense account! Can you imagine?"

Tiffany nodded, cracked a crab claw, and sucked on it.

Realizing she was not nearly as excited as he was, Thump paused. "What?"

"Nothing," she said. "I'm proud of you. I really am."

"But?"

"What if they don't let you in on managing this big trust? What if you don't get another promotion?"

"They'll have to." He took a deep breath, exhaling loudly. "I know what I'm dealing with."

"A bunch of white guys?"

"They are white, that's true. All the partners, but that could work in my benefit."

"How?"

"You see, they all have degrees from fancy schools, they have rich friends, and they mingle in social circles I can only dream of. But I have my own strengths." Thump counted on his fingers. "I'm persistent, proactive, and personable. I may not have gold-frame diplomas on the walls of my office, but I can connect with people. Anyway I can, I establish a connection. And each connection is the beginning of a relationship. First it's a personal relationship, then a professional relationship. It's harder to say no to someone you've been close with for a long time. That's why they have promoted me again and again."

"Isn't there a difference? Maybe they're fine with you as an employee, but making you their partner would be very different, wouldn't it?"

"They like me as an employee, they really do, and eventually they'll need a black partner to show they're open to diversity. And I'll be there, ready to step up. It's just a matter of time. And the Boulder Trust assignment could cut the time—"

"What if they don't put you on the trust team?"

"I'm hedging my risks. Not only within KKG or its existing clients. I'm hunting prospects any way possible. I'm calling potential clients, like doctors and business people. I'm even making house calls—"

"And joining gyms in fancy neighborhoods."

"That's right!" He laughed.

Tiffany smiled. "You're so driven, and I love that, but I worry that you—"

"You don't have to worry. I'm going to make lots of money at KKG, no matter what these folks do to help me or not."

"Money isn't everything."

"Says who? I grew up with no money, Mom making seven bucks an hour—and that's when she could find work. Trust me, money is a good thing, and more money is even better."

She played with a crab claw, pushing it around. "Won't buy you love."

"I already got love."

Tiffany smiled.

"Do you know what I thought of when Mr. Kolbe announced my promotion?"

"No." She took his hand. "Tell me."

"Try to guess." He clicked a finger at a waiter, who brought over an ice bucket with a bottle of champagne. "When Mr. Kolbe said that they're promoting me to vice president, what's the first thing that came to my mind?"

"Money?"

"No."

"A new car?"

"You're way off."

Tiffany held a finger to her lips, thinking. "I don't know. A bigger office? A prettier secretary?"

"What? You don't think Andy's pretty enough?"

They laughed, and Thump shook his head. "Maybe this will help you guess right." Kneeling down, he held forth a small box, opened it, and asked, "Will you marry me?"

Around them, patrons at the surrounding tables watched, smiling.

Tiffany looked at the ring, eyes wide. She hugged him, and they kissed.

The patrons broke into applause.

Gazing at the ring, Tiffany said, "It's really beautiful!"

"May I put it on your finger?"

"I haven't said yes yet."

"Then let me tell you what I thought the moment Mr. Kolbe promoted me."

She nodded.

"I thought of our future together. I imagined you and me, living together in a great house on a beautiful street with grass and trees and kids playing outside, including our kids. That's what I've been working for, what I've given everything to achieve."

"A perfect life?"

"Yes!"

Tiffany smiled. "I've been dreaming of it too. But there's something we need to discuss first."

Thump got off his knees, sat back in the chair, and leaned forward, close to her. "Talk to me, baby."

She hesitated. "If I say yes, I'll mean it. I'll be yours. I'll take care of you—"

"Me too, baby. Me too!"

"For me, it will be you—and only you. Can you promise the same?"

Thump opened his arms, as if the answer was obvious.

"Then swear to me. Take a vow that you'll never touch another woman."

Pressing a hand to his heart, Thump dropped back on his knees. "I, Thurgood Marshall Jefferson, being of sound body and mind, hereby take this vow to never, ever touch another woman, well, other than a casual hello, a peck on the cheek, stuff like that—"

Tiffany laughed.

"—so help me God!"

"Thank you." Tiffany held out her hand, and Thump slipped the engagement ring on her finger. They both looked at it for a long moment, then kissed again.

He popped the champagne, poured it, and raised the glass. "To our future! Success, health, and happiness!"

"Amen." Tiffany emptied her glass, watching him do the same.

He filled their glasses again. "No pressure, but since I'm not allowed to stay overnight with you in the nurses' dorms, what do you say about us looking for an apartment together?"

CHAPTER 14

The real estate agent, Mr. Soyer, was a white man, about forty, with an earnest air of someone who was determined to be well liked. He took Thump and Tiffany to see an apartment in the Mount Vernon area. It was a large prewar condominium with a high ceiling, dark wood floors, and single-pane windows.

"The molding," Mr. Soyer pointed, "is characteristic of that era. Attention to detail is absolutely incredible. They don't build like this anymore, and the rent is quite reasonable for the size and location. If I was in the market for a classy place with Old World charm, I'd snap this one up right now."

Thump looked at Tiffany, who shook her head.

"No problem," Mr. Soyer said. "We're moving on."

The next place was around the corner. It was another stately building with aged grandeur and a creaky, wood-paneled elevator that took them to the eighth floor.

"Very reasonable rent for this one." Mr. Soyer unlocked a heavy oak door. "It's got four bedrooms, three baths, and the address is highly sought after."

He entered and flipped a light switch. "This is charming."

Tiffany peeked in. The anteroom had three sets of tall glass doors that led to a sitting room, a dining room, and a library.

"The bedrooms," Mr. Soyer said, "are accessible through the sitting room."

Tiffany crinkled her nose. "What's that smell?"

"Let me open the windows," Mr. Soyer said. "Wait until you see the rest."

Thump glanced at Tiffany, saw her expression, and said, "I think this place is too claustrophobic."

"No problem," the agent said. "It's all part of the process."

They followed him in Thump's Mini. Approximately fifteen minutes north, they pulled into a cluster of new buildings with a secure underground garage and a silent elevator.

Entering a high-floor vacant apartment, Mr. Soyer led them straight to the balcony. "Look over there!" He pointed. "It's the Johns Hopkins University main campus. And over there," he said, almost yelling, shifting his aim, "Memorial Stadium, the old Orioles ball park."

"What's all this noise?" Tiffany looked over the railing. Below was an outdoor swimming pool and several wooden cabanas. A line of young trees and a concrete wall separated the pool area from a busy four-lane road.

Thump looked at her, she tapped her ears, and he started gesturing with his hands in an imitation of sign language, making her laugh.

Seeing this, Mr. Soyer smiled and beckoned them to follow him.

Twenty minutes later, they were taking an elevator to a sixth-floor apartment at the Harbor Towers. The apartment was new and empty, with honey-colored wood floors and plenty of sunlight.

Standing at the huge windows, even Mr. Soyer was speechless. Spread before them was the Inner Harbor, dotted with boats, and, across the water, downtown Baltimore.

Tiffany broke the silence with one word. "Wow!"

"Wow it is!" Thump shaded his eyes with his hand. "And you can see my office. Over there!"

"Let me show you the rest," Mr. Soyer said, leading them. "A stunning master bedroom here, with its own bathroom. Two bedrooms for guests, or for kids, should you have any."

"You bet we will," Thump said, and Tiffany pushed him playfully.

"And here," Mr. Soyer said, opening a door off the hallway, "is another full bathroom, which is a lot more practical than the traditional powder room. Like the rest of the apartment, it's equipped with premium fixtures, granite countertops, the works!"

They stopped at Mr. Soyer's office, where Thump signed the lease, wrote a check for the first month's rent and security deposit, and received two sets of keys. Mr. Soyer, delighted to close a deal, accompanied them to the door.

"Congratulations!" He shook hands with both of them. "Enjoy the rest of your Saturday."

As they settled back in the Mini, Thump dropped one set of keys in Tiffany's hand. She kissed him, a slow and long kiss. When she finally broke it off, still cradling his face in her hands, she said, "Thank you."

"For following your lead?"

She nodded.

"Thank my mother." Thump grinned. "She instructed me to carefully watch your reaction to each apartment, no matter how subtle the signs were and, at the first hint of displeasure, take the place off the list, good deal or not."

"She's a wise woman."

"Did I do well?"

"So far." Tiffany kissed him again. "But, you know, it's a big apartment and—"

"—and someone's got to furnish it," he finished the sentence for her.

"That's right!"

"You got it. But here's an idea: while it's empty, let's have an engagement party!"

Tiffany hesitated. "Most of my friends are in Tennessee."

"But this is home now, right?"

"Yes, it is." She pulled her phone from her purse and checked the calendar. "I'm not working Thursday night."

Thump pronounced each word as he was typing it on his phone. "Dear Colleagues and Friends, Come celebrate our engagement with us on Thursday, seven-thirty p.m.. Our new address is—"

Tiffany held up the copy of the lease Thump had just signed. "Harbor Towers, number six-oh-two."

CHAPTER 15

They attended Sunday morning services with Mrs. Jefferson at an all-black Baptist church. When the congregation sang "Jesus Loves You," Thump leaned over and whispered in Tiffany's ear, "I love you too." She laughed and covered her face when his mother gave them an admonishing glance.

After church, they had an early lunch at the Double T diner, then drove back to the church to drop Mrs. Jefferson off for a Bible study meeting.

Thump went around the car to open the door for his mother.

"That was a lovely morning," Mrs. Jefferson said as she was getting out of the Mini. "What are you kids doing the rest of the day?"

From the tight back seat, Tiffany said, "How about shopping for a bigger car?"

"Great idea!" Thump kissed his mom. "Now you understand why I love this girl?"

The Audi saleswoman, who saw them arrive in the Mini, first showed them a two-seater TT that sat on an elevated platform in the showroom.

"Excuse me," Tiffany asked, "where's the back seat?"

Thump's laughter quickly faded as he watched the two of them cross the showroom floor toward a bulky SUV. The saleswoman brought over a child car seat and showed Tiffany how easily it could be strapped in the second, and then the third row of seats.

"Uh-uh!" Thump quickly got out of the TT. "This is not happening!" He jogged over to a black S5 convertible. "Look at this one!"

She was standing behind the SUV, its rear door rising, while the saleswoman was explaining something about the trunk.

"Tiff!" He beckoned her over. "Tiffany!"

She signaled him to wait a minute while listening to the saleswoman.

Thump hurried over to the SUV, pulled out the car seat, brought it over, and fit it in the back seat of the S5. "Isn't that nice?"

Tiffany's expression said it all. She was not impressed.

Turning to the saleswoman, Thump said, "How about another child car seat?"

"No problem." She brought a second one over and strapped it in beside the first one. "The car is equipped with side-impact airbags for the rear seat occupants, not that you ever want to experience it, but it's good to know they're there, just in case."

Tiffany opened the passenger door and got in. She used the power controls to adjust the seat in several ways until it was comfortable.

"You want to know what's my favorite feature?" The saleswoman leaned over the side to indicate a set of switches. "Heated seats. I don't know how people used to live without them!"

An hour later, having test-driven an S5 and negotiated lease terms, Thump was signing a pile of papers while Tiffany watched. When he finished, he passed them back to the finance manager—a young man with a quick smile.

"Excellent." The finance manager flipped through the papers. "We'll submit the registration papers to the DMV. You should receive the permanent registration in the mail. Would you like to transfer your vanity license plate from the Mini?"

"Of course," Thump said.

Tiffany cleared her throat. "Really?"

CHAPTER 16

Monday morning, after their workout, Thump kissed Tiffany good-bye in front of the gym. She was in her nurse's uniform, he in a charcoal pinstripe suit and a red tie.

Hurrying toward the hospital, Tiffany turned and yelled, "Good luck!"

He blew her a kiss and walked the other way. As he approached the new S5, he stopped to admire it. His eyes were drawn to the license plate, which now read: *Goody!*

With the top open and rap music blasting, Thump drove off.

After stopping at McDonald's, he had fun on the 83 Freeway, weaving between cars with ease while keeping an eye out for police cruisers.

At the corner of Lombard and Charles Street, he stopped to hand the McDonald's tray to the homeless man, who paused and looked at the new car.

"Your blessings worked," Thump said. "Success!"

"Health and happiness," the homeless man mumbled, walking away. "Health and happiness. Yes, yes, yes."

At the office, Andy joined Thump in the office with a note pad. "I'm ready to start. What's the plan?"

"Board meeting is on Friday, but Sharon Boulder wants to review the presentation on Thursday. That gives us three full days to get the job done. We better boogie."

"Shoot," Andy said, his pencil ready over the pad. "Do you want me to draft the language?"

"No. I'll write the text for the PowerPoint slides. You'll do the research. Find me good companies to recommend investing in—"

"Good in what way?"

Thump considered the question for a moment. "Huggable companies, like green energy, recycling, shit like that."

"Got it." Andy wrote it down. "How about banks that give microloans to minority entrepreneurs?"

"That's good stuff, yes. And, you know, clothing brands or sneakers manufacturers that make crap in poor countries but cleaned up their act, like child labor, workers' safety—"

"Gay rights?"

Thump shook a finger at him. "Don't push it, girl!"

"Push what?" Andy made like he was ballet dancing to the door. "Anything else?"

"Don't transfer any calls, except from Tiffany and my mom. And track the RSVPs for the engagement party."

"No problem."

"One more thing," Thump said. "Don't leave me alone with Miss Kingman."

For the next few hours, Thump sat at his desk, typing furiously on his laptop while Andy brought over page after page of data about companies that fit the "goodness" criteria. For lunch, Andy ordered a noodle dish from a Chinese takeout restaurant.

Thump took a break from typing and reviewed Andy's research while slurping noodles with chopsticks. Andy came in with two more sheets of paper, which he added to the pile on Thump's desk. A little later, he showed up with a tall cup of coffee and cleared away the empty lunch container.

"Thanks," Thump said. "You're spoiling me."

"Oh please." Andy fluttered his eyelids in exaggerated feminine modesty. "It's my pleasure, boss."

"Go away," Thump said, laughing.

Thump sipped coffee while working his way through the rest of the research pile. He pulled out the companies he wanted to use as examples in the presentation. As he returned to typing more text for the slides, a knock on the door made him turn.

It was Henrietta Kingman.

"Look who's working hard," she said.

"And having fun!" Thump gestured at the papers. "We found some fascinating prospects."

"You did?" Kingman kicked the door closed with her high heel shoe. She pulled a pin, releasing her hair, and fluffed it around her shoulders. "How fascinating?"

"Highly fascinating!"

"That's good, but we don't want our new vice president working too hard."

"I'm enjoying it." Thump remained seated while she approached. He picked up one of the research articles. "This company, for example—"

Kingman took the paper from his hand and dropped it back on the desk. "Don't worry about the presentation too much."

"Are you kidding? This is my chance to—"

"Chance has nothing to do with it. Your career is my concern. Haven't I taken good care of you?"

"Absolutely. No question about it. You've been amazing. I'm totally grateful."

"That's good." She leaned on his shoulder. "Gratitude is the most important trait for a young man with big dreams."

"You're right. And I am grateful, totally grateful. But now that I'm engaged, we need to stop—"

"How adorable." Kingman massaged his bicep muscles. "You try so hard."

"No, really. I promised her—"

"Promises, promises." With both hands, Kingman held his head and tilted it back to make him look up at her. "It's just the two of us here, naughty boy, and you're making me so hot—"

The door flew open and Andy entered. "Mr. Jefferson—"

Kingman stepped away from Thump.

Seeing them, Andy stumbled and dropped a bunch of papers.

"Gee," Thump said, "what happened to knocking?"

"I'm sorry!" Andy started collecting the papers. "I'm really sorry."

Thump got up and went over to help him.

"Well then." Kingman headed for the door. "Let me know if you need more help."

"Thanks," Thump said. "Appreciate it!"

When she was gone, he said to Andy, "What took you so long?"

"I was in the bathroom."

"At the wrong time, obviously."

"I had to go." Andy put the papers on the desk. "Should I wear diapers tomorrow?"

"Very funny." Thump thought for a moment. "You know, I have an idea."

An hour later, they were settled in a glass-walled conference room, each at his laptop. Andy had set up a portable printer and arranged all the research papers on the large table in neat piles. They could hear the phones ring in the reception area down the hall, as well as the voices of employees chatting in the kitchenette next door. Every few minutes someone passed in the hallway, glancing into the conference room.

"This is weird," Andy said. "I feel like a fish in an aquarium."

Thump chuckled. "Would you rather be a fish in the ocean? With all the sharks?"

"I'd rather not be a fish at all."

"What's wrong with being a fish?"

Feigning anger, Andy said, "Why do I have to be a fish? I don't want to live in this aquarium!"

"What could be better than being a fish in an aquarium?"

"A faggot in Baltimore, that would be better."

Thump threw his head back and hollered in laughter until tears came to his eyes.

Out in the hallway, a group of secretaries holding coffee cups stopped and watched.

CHAPTER 17

Early on Tuesday morning, a garbage truck was working its way up Lombard Street when Thump stopped at the curb. He got out of the car and carried the McDonald's tray with coffee and a sandwich across the sidewalk, where he put it down next to the sleeping homeless man.

A few minutes later, at the large table in the glass-walled conference room, Thump sat with his back to the hallway. He worked through the morning, typing data into his laptop while Andy, seated on the opposite side of the table, continued his research.

Shortly before noon, Andy said, "Kingman just passed by, checked us out."

"Good," Thump said. "She won't come back for a while, and I'm getting hungry."

Andy left. A half hour later he returned with sandwiches in a brown bag and two bottles of iced tea, which they consumed while working.

It was midafternoon when Kingman returned. This time, she walked into the conference room. "Is this the new command center?"

"It is." Thump stopped typing, but kept his fingers above the keys. "How are you?"

She looked at Andy. "Be a sweetheart, fetch me a bottle of water, will you?"

"Of course, Miss Kingman." Andy got up, glanced at Thump, and left.

Looking over Thump's shoulder at the laptop, she asked, "Making good progress?"

"About halfway through the first draft. Lots to go still."

"How about a little break?"

"Not now." He blew air. "I'm in the zone, you know?"

"That's not a problem. I'll put you back in the zone afterward."

He moved his fingers over the keyboard as if he was typing. "Flowing real good, momentum, train of thought, that kind of thing. If I stop, it'll be a pain to restart."

"You're too serious." She curled a finger. "Come, a bit of R and R won't hurt your momentum."

"Wish I could, but time is tight. Mr. Kolbe expects a top-notch presentation."

Kingman's expression remained friendly, but her hoarse voice had an edge. "Mr. Kolbe always relies on my judgment—"

She paused as several employees walked down the hallway. Thump waved at them through the glass wall.

When they were gone, he said, "How about tomorrow afternoon? I'll have most of the presentation done. Would love to hear your input."

Andy returned with a water bottle.

Kingman took the bottle. "Thanks." She smiled at Thump. "I'll see you at two p.m. tomorrow in my office."

After Kingman left, Thump said to Andy, "Listen, tomorrow after lunch, at one thirty or so, but not before, pass word to the assistants of Mr. Kolbe, Goldberg, and Chang that I'll be showing a draft of the PowerPoint presentation in Henrietta Kingman's office at two p.m. sharp. Got it?"

Andy sat down, shaking his head. "Here comes trouble."

"No trouble. I have it under control. Let's concentrate on the presentation. Do you have any new prospects for me?"

"Actually, I do." Andy handed him a sheet of paper. "Look at this company: Rye's Poultry. It has over a hundred million dollars in annual sales, all free range, using no cages, no antibiotics, no hormones."

"That's what I'm looking for! How about organic food growers, suppliers?"

"I'm looking. There's a bunch of them, but most aren't very attractive, financially speaking. Margins are tiny in the food business, so the projections aren't impressive. But some of these companies are truly conscientious about the environment—"

"Don't give me any tree huggers."

"They're not tree huggers," Andy said, "but it's kind of hard to balance being good and being profitable."

"Story of my life." Thump held up the Rye's Poultry sheet. "Anyway, we need winners. The whole goodness strategy is about image, fluff. Free chickens running around the range are very cute, but the companies we recommend for the trust to invest in must show solid business and market share, strong management teams, conservative finances, and great five-year projections. We're looking for rising stock values, not charity cases."

It was dark when Thump left the office. Driving away from the KKG building, he lowered the volume on the sound system and called Tiffany.

She answered after four rings. "I was just thinking about you."

"I think about you all the time," he said.

"Oh, you are smooth!"

Thump started singing, "Love is in the air—"

Tiffany laughed. "Why are you in the car so late?"

"Work. I'm showing the presentation to the partners tomorrow."

"I'm sure they'll love it." She paused. "Oops. A patient's buzzing me. Got to go. Love you!"

"Love you too," he said.

CHAPTER 18

On Wednesday, at 2:00 p.m. in Henrietta Kingman's office, the curtains were drawn and the projector showed the first slide of the presentation. Seated on the white sofa and armchairs were Mr. Kolbe, Arthur Goldberg, and Bo Chang. Henrietta Kingman stood by the wall, arms folded across her chest.

The first slide showed the title of the presentation:

Boulder Trust – Strategic Plan
Prepared by KKG Investments, Inc.
T.M. Jefferson, VP

"This is still a draft," Thump said. "I'm open to your comments and suggestions, anything at all, either substantive or style, go ahead and tell me."

Tapping the arrow key on his laptop, he moved to the second slide: *Introduction.*

"The intro covers the basic premise of this proposed investment strategy, which is nothing short of a new paradigm for managing the principal funds of nonprofit organizations. Under this new strategy, social and charitable goals will be promoted not only by handing over donations and grants to nonprofit charities but by investing the trust's principal funds in likeminded, for-profit, virtuous companies."

"I like it," Mr. Kolbe said. "Virtuous companies. It's catchy!"

"A catchy oxymoron," Goldberg said.

"That's why it's so catchy," Chang said.

Everyone laughed.

Thump moved to the next slide. “Here’s an excellent example for an investment prospect: Solar Eclipso, based in Nevada but does all its manufacturing in Mexico, where the company sponsors a school for workers’ children and a community center for the elderly.” He used a pointer to highlight the financial tables. “Five-year projections for dividends and stock prices will give the trust double-digit annual returns on every dollar invested—”

“And a hefty bonus for us,” Chang said.

Thump flipped through the succeeding slides while explaining, “I chose companies in different categories: energy, agriculture, food, technology, biotech, health, communications, manufacturing, transportation, and construction. Each one validates our basic premise—”

“Very good.” Mr. Kolbe got up and pulled open the curtains to let in daylight. “This is how you can turn an original and clever idea into a serious plan of implementation.”

“Thank you,” Thump said. “If you have any questions—”

Goldberg and Chang shook their heads.

“I have a question.” Kingman’s voice was more hoarse than usual. “Why the blanks in some of your projection tables? The numbers are missing.”

“We have the numbers,” Thump said. “Didn’t have time to put everything in, but we have all the figures handy, ready to go in. It will all be done by tomorrow.”

“Excellent,” Mr. Kolbe said, clapping his big hands so loudly that everyone jolted. “Fill in the rest of the numbers, and you have a winner here!”

As they all got up to leave, Goldberg said, “I heard O’Connor is calling around to other trust beneficiaries, trying to drum up support for her client’s opposition to our management contract.”

“That’s true,” Kingman said. “And she sent Sharon Boulder a written demand to be on the agenda and be allowed to address the board directly.”

“I see.” Mr. Kolbe turned to the window and gazed outside for a long moment. “She’s becoming a real problem. What do we know about her?”

"As far as I recall," Goldberg said, "O'Connor was a highly effective judge until she resigned suddenly without an explanation."

"That's interesting." Kingman cleared her throat. "Let's find out why she resigned. If it's ugly enough, we can use it."

"Use it?" Chang asked. "How?"

"Doesn't matter," Mr. Kolbe said. "We won't be involved. John Davis will deal with the details. He'll find out what happened and tip his media contacts."

"The media?" Goldberg paused, looking at them. "It could ruin her."

"She started this war," Kingman said. "It's only fair that she suffers the consequences."

CHAPTER 19

Thump was busy disconnecting his laptop from the projector when he heard the door lock click. Everyone had left Kingman's office but him.

"Finally," she said, "I have you all to myself."

Rolling up the wires, Thump forced a smile on his face. "Even I don't have myself to myself. I'll be lucky to finish this presentation in time—"

"If I didn't know better," she said, approaching him, "I'd think you're trying to avoid me."

"It's not that, but you know, me and Tiffany, we are now—"

"I'm genuinely happy for you." Kingman reached behind and loosened her skirt button. "For me, starting a family wasn't possible, with my work and all the things I had to do to get ahead. But you're a man, you can have both."

"You don't mind?"

"Why would I mind?" She stood very close to him. "It's a wonderful thing. I read in *Business Week* that research shows that married men are more successful in their careers and also live longer."

Thump finished packing up his laptop. "Tiffany made me swear that I will not—"

"What's she got to do with us?" Kingman started undoing Thump's belt.

He held her hands to stop her. "Please. I'm committed to Tiffany."

Kingman looked at him, her eyes narrowing. "What's so special about her?"

"Tiffany?" He chuckled. "She's very special."

"Young?" Kingman snorted. "Pretty? Sexy?"

"She is all that, yes, but that's not why I want her to be my wife." He paused, thinking. "It's because she's pure, all good. She's totally honest. Totally. I've never met anyone like that before."

"I'm sure she's a sweet girl." Kingman pushed his hand away and resumed undoing his belt. "But did she hire a C student from a state school?"

He tried to stop her, and she pushed his hand away again.

"Did she give the chance of a lifetime to an MBA dropout?"

He gave up on trying to stop her from undoing his belt.

"Did she teach you how to dress? How to speak? How to read balance sheets?"

"No, but she—"

"That's right. She didn't." Kingman unzipped him roughly. "Did she promote you again and again till you're a thumping VP at the most exclusive firm in town?"

"Please, stop!" Thump grabbed her hands. "She's my fiancée!"

Kingman tried to respond, but started coughing hard.

He held her. "Are you OK?"

"I'm fine," she said and coughed a few more times. "Look, I don't want to argue with you."

"Same here. I'm trying to do the right thing—"

"Lots of successful businessmen, wonderful husbands, have fun on the side. It's part of office life. Everybody knows that."

"But I promised to be exclusive—"

"What she doesn't know can't hurt her." Kingman shoved her hand into his pants. "If God wanted you to be exclusive, he would not have endowed you with this."

A series of knocks came from the door.

"I'm in a meeting!" Kingman moved her hand back and forth inside Thump's pants.

More knocks came from the door.

"Not now," Kingman yelled. "I'm busy!"

There was a brief silence outside. Then another knock.

Kingman reluctantly pulled out her hand and went to the door. “What’s the problem?”

Thump quickly zipped up and buckled his belt.

“Miss Kingman?” It was Andy’s voice. “It’s an emergency!”

She unlocked the door and threw it open. “What emergency?”

“Mr. Jefferson!” Andy came in. “Your mother is on the phone! She must talk to you immediately!”

Thump grabbed his laptop and ran to the door. “My mom? What the hell—”

Back at the conference room, Thump put down his laptop and dropped in the chair. “That was a close call.”

“She’s going to fire me,” Andy said.

“Over my dead body.”

“Will that stop her?”

“Don’t worry about it. Once the Boulder Trust’s board adopts my plan, it’ll be a whole new ballgame. She’s going to leave me alone.”

“Still two days to go.”

“You know what?” Thump glanced at his watch. “I’m going to work at home. Help me pack up the papers.”

CHAPTER 20

In the new apartment, Thump sat on a barstool at the kitchen counter, sifting through the research papers and typing in the data. The windows had been dark for hours, and he was getting tired.

On the wall-mounted TV, the eleven o'clock news came on. He glanced up and recognized the photo of a woman wearing a judge's robe.

"Based on a reliable source," said a TV reporter, "Judge Ruth O'Connor resigned from the court six months ago after allegedly making racist remarks to a colleague, who complained to the chief judge. According to our source, the following were O'Connor's exact words."

Thump unscrewed the cap from a bottle of water while words appeared under O'Connor's photo and the TV reporter quoted her.

"I'm tired of sending African American men to jail. Let's address the underlying cause: the black culture of victimhood, entitlement, and animosity toward whites. This culture creates a false justification for pathological social dysfunction and disregard for the law. Especially among young inner city African Americans, it's a culture of violence, drugs, rapes, and primal seed-spreading that results in countless out-of-wedlock children."

Thump gulped water while the screen switched back to the reporter, who said: "Former Judge O'Connor has since returned to practicing law. One of her first clients is the West Virginia Freedom League, an organization dedicated to glorifying the Confederate Army and its fight to prolong slavery and subjugation of African Americans."

CHAPTER 21

In the morning, O'Connor's husband, Jerald, drove her to the office. He dropped her off before going to park the car, and she crossed the sidewalk toward the entrance to the building. The street level was taken by an establishment called The Bar Bar, a watering hole popular with courtroom lawyers—divorce, criminal defense, and personal injury attorneys.

She paused to look at the directory by the front door, which listed about twenty businesses. The bottom one, freshly painted, read: *R. O'Connor, Esq. – Law Office.*

"Judge O'Connor?"

She turned to see a TV reporter and a cameraman.

"Good morning, Judge. Will you comment on the recent allegations?"

O'Connor opened the door. "My only comment is that I'm no longer a judge, so don't call me that. Good day!"

"Are you a racist?"

She paused. "That's a defamatory question."

"It's a simple question," he said. "Are you a racist? Yes or no?"

"What's a racist?"

"Saying bad things about blacks."

O'Connor turned to face him. "Like saying that one-third of African American men are in trouble with the law? That they have the highest incarceration rates of any ethnic or racial group?"

"Is that really—"

"How about saying that more black men go to prison than to college?"

"Racial discrimination in courts and universities isn't new—"

"Saying that black men kill, and are being killed by black men, at a per-capita rate many times greater than any other group? That the same distinction appears in sex crimes and property crimes?"

"If these facts are true—"

"They are true! And so is the fact that only thirty percent of adult blacks are married and that seventy percent of black children are born to mothers out of wedlock." O'Connor glared at him. "Saying these things make me a racist?"

"I'd say." He glanced at his cameraman to make sure the exchange was being filmed.

"Then the US Census Bureau and the Bureau of Justice Statistics are also racist," O'Connor said. "In fact, reality itself is racist. And if you dare repeat these factually correct statistics on the air, you'll be called racist too!" She turned and went inside the building.

CHAPTER 22

On Thursday, after a morning of intense work, Thump had sushi takeout for lunch—California roll and seaweed salad—while Andy connected the laptop to a projector aimed at a white screen that covered the only nonglass wall of the conference room.

"I should do another dry run." Thump tapped on his watch. "Mrs. Boulder will be here in twenty minutes."

Andy adjusted the focus on the projector. "It's ready to go."

"Here's what I need you to do." Thump tossed a set of keys to Andy. "Go to my apartment and wait for the caterers. They should be there around two to start preparing for the party. Tiffany's working till five, then going to her place to get ready."

"I'll take care of it."

"Make sure they set up some tables and chairs. The place has no furniture yet. I also ordered flowers and—"

"I have the list." Andy held up a sheet of paper. "Good luck with Mrs. Boulder."

Andy left, and Thump started reviewing the PowerPoint slides, taking his time to read silently through the text on each one.

Halfway through, the phone rang.

He hit the speaker button. "Yes?"

"Mr. Jefferson?" It was the receptionist. "Sharon Boulder called. She's not feeling well and asked that the meeting take place at her house instead of at our office."

“Her house? No. That’s not good.” Thump cursed silently. “Get her on the line for me, will you?”

“Actually, she asked that we don’t call back. She’s resting. Come over in one hour, she said.”

CHAPTER 23

Thump pulled into Boulder's long driveway in his Audi, top down, basking in the sunshine. He turned down the music and proceeded slowly up the gravel path toward the massive stone mansion, followed the circular driveway around a water fountain, and stopped by the front steps.

Farther around the circle, Ricardo was dusting the limo with a long brush, which he raised in a casual gesture of welcome. Thump waved back.

Sharon Boulder opened the front door. She wore tight pink shorts and a matching exercise bra, her hair collected in girly pigtails. She took him by the arm and led him to a living room with rainbow upholstery and fresh flowers in vases. The windows were open, letting in the sounds of birds chirping and a distant lawnmower.

Thump kept his jacket on as they sat together on a sofa. He fired up his laptop and started going through the presentation, first the introduction, then the individual examples of particular investment prospects. She listened with frequent approving nods.

"This company is my favorite." Thump pointed to the screen. "They build low-income housing from recycled building materials. The lower costs of supplies and the subsidies from local government and the US Department of Energy inflate profit margins to almost double those of direct competitors—"

"Fantastic." She reached over and closed the laptop. "This is wonderful."

"Wait, I'm not done." Thump tried to reopen the laptop.

"Yes you are." She took it from him and put it on a side table. "I've seen all I need to see."

"But there's a whole section about how this strategy will generate value, how the Boulder Trust will experience positive growth—"

"You're excited over all these numbers—how cute!" She leaned on him, clasping his thigh. "The presentation is perfect. Just like you."

"Do you have any questions or comments? I still have time to revise before tomorrow's board meeting."

"Comments?" She held a finger to her lip as a little girl would do while thinking. "I know! Why don't you put the logo of each company on the relevant slide? It'll add color, make it warmer, like spring. There's always growth in the spring, isn't there?"

"Great idea." Thump stood up. "I'll do it. Well then, I better be going—"

"Fix us a couple of drinks, will you?" She pointed to the bar.

While he scooped ice, she came over, pressed her body to him from behind, and felt him with her hands. "You're so firm all over, like an Arabian stallion."

Thump turned to her with the drinks. "I wanted to share with you something personal."

"Already heard the news." She took the glass and raised it. "Congratulations on your engagement!"

"Thank you." He clicked glasses with her. "The thing is, I made a commitment to be—"

"Exclusive. I heard that too."

"You have?"

"That girl is very lucky." Sharon Boulder gulped a good half of her drink.

Taking a quick sip, Thump asked, "So you're OK with it?"

"Young love. It's so romantic." She finished her drink. "I still remember my first boyfriend, how we felt about each other, what we did together—couldn't stop doing. I remember everything like it was yesterday. We were in love, crazy about each other. Crazy. And he wanted to marry me, even got a cheap ring at the local pawnshop. But he was nineteen, and he had nothing. I didn't want to stay poor for the rest of my life. Love dies very quickly when you're poor."

He emptied his glass.

"Then I met Hank." She poured herself another drink. "His first wife died after a long illness, his kids were grown up, and he needed someone like me. It wasn't young love, not by a long shot. But it wasn't dead either. It was adult love, of mutual interests, stable, with deep feelings and all that. He was a perfect gentleman, kind and generous and classy. Yes, Hank had class, and I had youth and beauty." She poked Thump in the chest. "Just like you."

He put his drink down. "Thank you."

"You have my blessing." She raised her glass again. "Honestly, Girl Scout's honor, I want you to be happy."

"Thank you. It means a lot to me."

"And you mean a lot to me." She massaged his chest muscles, kissed his neck. "You're a lot of fun, not like all the stuffy types I meet at those cultural events."

Thump tried to move away, but she held on.

"How does the song go?" Sharon Boulder looked up at the ceiling, trying to remember. "*Once you go black, you never go back.*"

He shook his head. "That's such a cliché."

"But it's true!" She kissed his neck again. "You're better than any other man I have ever been with—not that I've been with a lot of guys, but you know what I mean, right?"

"I'm not the only black guy around."

"Oh my God! You're so bad!" She laughed and touched his face with an open hand as if slapping him. "Now you have to stay!"

Thump took a couple of steps toward the door.

"Don't rush." She followed him. "I'm not a strong person, you understand, not as strong as you are, to jump off the wagon like this, while we're still moving."

"I'm sorry. I really am, but—"

"I've gotten used to you. I can trust you, enjoy you without worrying, you understand?"

"Please, I really need to go."

"One last time. Is that too much to ask?"

He stepped back, away from her. "I can't. Please understand."

Following him, she purred and shook her pigtails. “How about we call it breakup sex?”

“Mrs. Boulder—”

“Sharon.”

“Sharon, please, I’m asking you to respect—”

“Oh, by the way, Henrietta told me they made you VP.”

Taken aback by the change of subject, Thump nodded.

“Congratulations on that too.”

“Thank you.”

“Did you realize,” she said sweetly, “that the letters VP could also stand for Very Poor?”

The words smacked Thump hard. He turned away from her, his face contorting, his chest struggling to expand for a deep breath to fight off a wave of nausea.

“Baby, don’t be sad.” She rubbed his back. “I only want to have some fun, you and me, here and there, a little action, in private. We’ll be discreet, like always.”

Even through his shirt and suit, her hand on his back felt hard and prodding. He flexed his hands, his nausea turning to anger.

“You’re the same as I was, back then,” she said, “thirty years ago. Smart, sexy, going for it, getting what I wanted, no matter what I had to do. And it’s worth it! Look at this house! Don’t you want to own a house like this one day?”

He didn’t answer.

“We’re the same. That’s why I understand you.” Her hand descended to his butt, and she scratched it with her long fingers. “It’s our secret. Nobody knows, nobody cares, right?”

He clenched his fists, knuckling one against the other.

Perhaps she felt his anger, because she stopped scratching his butt. “Come on, I’m like melted butter in there. We’ll make it quick. A thump to remember. What do you say?”

He exhaled, nodded, and reached into his pocket, fishing out a Bull-M condom.

“Woo hoo!” Sharon Boulder lowered her shorts, turned, and bent over, resting her elbows on the bar counter. On her excited face, the skin seemed as tight as parchment. At the sound of him tearing the condom wrapper, she bit her lower lip expectantly.

In the circular driveway in front of the Boulder mansion, Ricardo swung the long brush, sweeping across the long roof of the limo when a terrible scream came through the open windows.

Ricardo froze in shock.

The scream repeated, now recognizable as Mrs. Boulder's voice. "Ahhhhh!"

Still holding the brush, he ran to the front door, threw it open, and stepped inside, where he heard her again.

"Fucking animal! You're in my ass! My aaaaaaass!"

Ricardo hesitated, unsure what to do.

"Don't! Don't come out! Don't you dare!"

Taking another step toward the source of the voice, Ricardo paused at hearing her next uttering.

"That's it! Slowly! Keep going!"

Ricardo hesitated.

"Yes! Nail me! Again! Again!"

Turning away, Ricardo stepped back outside.

"Ahhhh! Yes! That's it! Harder! Deeper! DEEPER!"

His face red, Ricardo closed the front door and descended the front steps while Mrs. Boulder could be heard through the windows.

"Yeah! Yeah! Yeah!" She was yelling it rhythmically, faster and faster. "Yeah! Yeah! Yeah! Yeah! Yeahhhhhhhh!"

Ricardo pulled back his arm and hurled the brush as far as he could over the circular driveway. It hit a tree and broke in half.

CHAPTER 24

The conference room windows had gradually darkened while Thump was working at his laptop, copying and pasting company logos onto the PowerPoint slides.

His mobile phone rang.

Tiffany's face appeared on the screen. She asked, "Where are you?"

"I have to finish up. The board meeting is first thing tomorrow morning, and I got comments from Mrs. Boulder that I have to put in."

"Hurry up."

"I'm trying, trust me. But this is it, today, tonight, whatever. Tomorrow morning, Boulder Trust will be my *Get Out of Jail* ticket. That's why I have to get this presentation right, make them so excited that they'll want me to manage the implementation, and then, I'm in the driver seat—"

"Just get here!" She lowered her voice to almost a whisper. "People are starting to arrive!"

"OK, baby. I'm almost done. Ten, twenty minutes max."

"That's too long. I can't be alone with them."

"They don't bite, I promise."

"I bite!"

"Ouch!" He laughed. "I'm on my way."

The last four slides went quickly, and he read aloud through the *Conclusions* page.

On the way out, Thump stopped by his office, left the laptop on his desk, grabbed his keys and suit jacket, and ran out the door.

When Thump entered his apartment, it was already full of guests—mostly white colleagues from KKG. Soft music was playing while white-gloved waiters walked around with silver trays of tiny appetizers.

Tiffany saw him and hurried over. She kissed him and said quietly, "I'm going to kill you!"

He put his lips to her ear and said, "Go ahead, I probably deserve it."

Goldberg and Chang came over to shake Thump's hand while the sound of tapping on glass made everyone quiet down.

"Ladies, gentlemen," Mr. Kolbe said. "May I have your attention, please?"

Hearing his deep, sonorous voice, the chattering ceased, and there was total silence.

"Thank you." He smiled. "Now that our gracious host has made his fashionably late entrance—"

The room exploded with laughter.

"On behalf of all of us at KKG," Mr. Kolbe continued, "as you two prepare to start a family, we wish you a long and steady union, blessed with good fortune and mutual joy."

Amid all the clapping, Thump and Tiffany beamed. He picked a glass from a tray. "Thank you, Mr. Kolbe. And this is to the partners and to all my colleagues at KKG." He raised the glass. "You gave me the courage to propose to the woman I love. For that I'll be grateful to you all forever. Thank you!"

Mr. Kolbe raised his glass again. "You're welcome, Mr. Jefferson."

The guests drank, and then someone started chanting, "Thump! Thump! Thump!"

Others joined, until the whole room went, "Thump! Thump! Thump! Thump! Thump!"

Tiffany raised her hands. "Excuse me! Excuse me! I want to—"

She waited, smiling, as they quieted down.

"I want to thank you for sharing in our happiness, and also to tell you a secret." She waited for total silence. "I don't like this nickname, Thump. From now on, can it be Goody?"

After some murmuring, the chanting resumed, but this time it was: "Goo-Dee! Goo-Dee! Goo-Dee! Goo-Dee!"

Pretending to be embarrassed, Thump buried his face in his hands.

The chanting petered out with laughs and clapping, and the guests resumed socializing. Thump and Tiffany locked in a slow, happy, loving kiss.

Andy came over, hugged Tiffany and shook Thump's hand. "What's the word, boss."

"Presentation's ready," Thump said. "I left the laptop on my desk. Get there early in the morning, set up the projector for the trust's board meeting in the conference room, and make sure it all works."

Tiffany, meanwhile, drifted away, shaking hands and making small talk.

"I'll get it ready," Andy said. "Will you be the one making the presentation to the trustees?"

"Of course he will." Henrietta Kingman surprised them from behind. "It's his presentation, or his execution, depending on how it goes." Seeing Thump's face, she elbowed him. "Don't worry. It'll be a smashing success."

He chuckled, relieved.

Andy's smile evaporated as soon as he turned away.

"Great apartment," Kingman said. "How about a tour?"

CHAPTER 25

After he showed her the bedrooms, while heading back up the hallway toward the living room, Thump knocked on the hallway bathroom and, hearing no response, opened the door. “Take a look at this,” he said. “It’s bigger than my mom’s living room.”

“This is a beautiful bathroom.” Kingman nudged him in and closed the door behind them. “Let’s try it on for size.”

“Oh no.” Thump tried to get past her to the door. “Please, don’t start.”

“Start what?” She blocked his way.

He reached behind her for the door handle.

“Uh-uh!” Kingman slapped his hand away and locked the door. “Be a good boy, or you won’t get any more candy.”

“The place is full of guests. Are you crazy?”

“Hey!” Kingman shook a finger at him. “Watch your language, young man!”

“Come on, you can’t expect me to—”

“Don’t tell me what to expect.” Kingman started to undo Thump’s belt. “No interruptions, no phone calls from Mom, no glass-walled conference rooms.”

“Please, don’t ask me to do this.”

“I’m not asking. I’m telling.” She unzipped him. “You thumped Sharon fucking Boulder—in the ass no less! Me you can do up front.” She pulled down his pants. “I like to see nature’s wonder, right up!”

Trying to turn away, he pleaded, “I can’t do it, really.”

“You can’t?” She grabbed his penis. “So what’s this for?”

In the crowded living room, Tiffany stood by the windows with Chang and Goldberg, who marveled at the view. Her eyes searched among the guests.

"Look," Goldberg said, "you can see *Steady Hands* from here. There, next to the aquarium. Mr. Kolbe bought it out of foreclosure five years ago."

Tiffany looked. "It's big."

"Have you been on it?"

She shook her head.

"It's incredible," Chang said. "It's our company's yacht, but according to the IRS, we're not supposed to take it out for personal pleasure, only for business purposes, like client development and so on. But it can be arranged, and Thump is the expert, if you know what I mean."

"What do you mean?" Goldberg said to Chang, and they laughed.

Her eyes drifted back to the room. "Do you know where Goody is?"

"Goody?" Chang looked at her, confused, then remembered. "Oh, Goody. It'll take me some time to get used to it."

Goldberg scanned the room. "I don't see him."

Kingman pulled on him with her hand, back and forth. "Here we go. Someone's waking up, coming to life, raising its gorgeous head."

"This is wrong." Thump looked up at the ceiling, shaking his head. "Wrong."

"Look, I understand things will have to change." She kept her hand moving. "They always do."

Thump looked at her, hopeful.

"But right now, your goal is success. That's all you think about. Success. Success. Success. Am I right?"

He nodded.

"Status, partnership, wealth—becoming rich!—that's what you want more than anything else, that's your biggest desire, correct?"

He nodded again.

"And my biggest desire right now is this." Kingman tugged on his penis, now fully erect. "Tit for tat."

A long sigh was all he managed.

She pulled her skirt up over her narrow hips and dropped her panties. "God, I'm totally soaked already." Raising herself backward onto the granite counter, her back to the mirror, she lifted her legs and hugged her knees. Hanging from her high-heeled shoe, the silk panties showed her monogram initials: *HDK*.

Thump ripped a condom wrapper with his teeth and slipped it on. He stepped forward between her upturned legs, felt his way for a moment, and thrust into her.

"My guess is," Goldberg said, "he's probably talking business with someone, chewing their ear about how great KKG is and how we can do better for their long-term investment portfolio."

"Probably," Chang agreed. "Did you invite any of the neighbors?"

"I didn't," Tiffany said, "but maybe he did. Making friends is easy for him. I'm not so good at that."

"I bet that's what he's doing." Goldberg said. "There's a lot of money in this apartment complex. And the Ritz-Carlton Residences next door? Talk about a treasure trove for the brazen marketer!"

"You're right." Chang laughed. "I can see him riding up and down the elevators, hitting on the neighbors. Before you know it, half of them will be his clients, knocking on your door every time the stock market has a hiccup."

"Day and night." Goldberg knocked on the window several times. "You better get used to it."

Tiffany smiled. "Will you excuse me for a moment?" She left the two KKG partners and made her way between the guests toward the other side of the room.

They watched her go, looked at each other, and Goldberg said, "Crap!"

In the bathroom, Thump was going at it, in and out, in and out, his eyes shut, his hands behind his back. Kingman watched him, her mouth gaping, letting out a choked yelp every time he pounded her. She leaned back, her shoulder blades against the mirror, her bent arms hooked around her upturned knees. The only physical contact between them was the hot friction of their genitals.

Tiffany walked between the guests, smiling, nodding, and searching. She peeked into the kitchen, which was busy with the catering staff. Thump was nowhere. She made her way to the hallway, down toward the bedrooms.

Breathing faster now, Thump paused. He raised his hands, reached forward on each side of Kingman's head, pressed his palms to the mirror behind her for support, and resumed thumping her, hard, harder, his eyes shut again, his skin slapping hers rhythmically, faster, and it sounded like *Thump! Thump! Thump!*

Tiffany peeked into the master bedroom, which was empty except for a mattress on the floor, made with sheets and a comforter. She looked into the second, empty bedroom. Andy was there, talking to a male waiter, their heads close. She smiled and moved on.

The hallway bathroom door was still closed. Tiffany knocked and tried the handle. It was locked. She listened, expecting whoever was inside to say something.

The knock on the door caused Thump to stop and open his eyes. He saw himself in the mirror, and his face twisted in pain. He jerked back as if he were electrocuted, his back hitting the wall behind.

Raising her hand to knock again, Tiffany paused as Chang and Goldberg came down the hallway in a hurry.

"Come quick," Chang said. "You got to see it! Come!"

She followed them toward the living room. "What's going on?"

"The aquarium," Goldberg said. "All the lights just came on. It's breathtaking!"

Thump regained his balance. Groaning, he tore off the condom and threw it into the toilet. Kingman, still on the counter with her knees up and wide open, took a few seconds to emerge from the fog of extreme arousal and realized he had moved away from her.

"Hey!" Her hoarse voice barely came through, rough as sandpaper. "Get back here!"

He pulled up his pants. "God, what have I done."

"I said, come back here!"

He quickly shoved his shirt tails into his pants, and when his hand touched his still-erect penis, he clenched a fist and hit it. "Idiot!" He hit it again. "Idiot! Idiot! Idiot!"

"Shut up!" Kingman's voice cleared up almost to its normal hoarseness. "Thump me! Now!"

He fumbled with his belt, struggling to thread it through the buckle.

She lowered her upturned legs, slipped off the counter, still breathing hard, and slapped him hard across the face. "I said, *Thump me*!"

Her slap shocked him. His eyes slowly focused on her.

"Do it!" Kingman slapped him again. "You stupid gorilla!"

He raised his hands, defending his face.

"Who do you think you are?" Her hands shaking, she tore open his belt and tried to pull down his pants. "Do it!"

Thump grasped the ends of his loose belt and held on, preventing her from pulling his pants down.

Growling in frustration, Kingman let go of his pants and slapped him again. And again.

He didn't try to defend his face anymore.

She slapped him one more time.

"I'm sorry," he said quietly. "I can't do this anymore."

"You can't thump me?" She reached up with both hands, clutched his ears, and pulled downward on both ears, hard.

"Ahh!" Thump tried to pull her hands off his ears, but she held tightly and he was forced to kneel before her.

"You don't want to use your dick?" Kingman pulled him by the ears toward her exposed vagina. "Then use your mouth, boy! Eat me!"

He tried to turn his head away, but she clutched his ears too tightly.

Lifting one leg to hook around him, she pressed herself to his face. "Eat me, boy!"

He struggled to turn his head away.

"Eat me!" She sank her nails into the back of his ears to prevent him from turning. "Eat!"

"No!" Thump grabbed her by the hips and swiveled her around, which tore her hands away from his ears. Rising from his kneeling position, he took hold of each of her thighs from behind, his large hands grasping the back of her knees, and lifted her while opening her legs wide.

Holding her up like this, Thump recreated Kingman's position from a moment ago, when she was getting thumped with her knees high, parted wide, panties hanging from one high-heeled shoe. But now she was held up in the air, facing the large mirror, her hair wild, her enraged face showing her age, and the inside of her thighs angry red.

"Look at yourself!" Thump shook her. "Look!"

After a moment of wide-eyed shock, Kingman gave a hoarse, guttural shriek and kicked wildly, which sent her panties flying from her shoe to the corner. She wriggled out of his arms, dropped to the floor, and crawled to the toilet bowl, where she convulsed and vomited.

Thump took a hand towel from a hook and placed it near her. He unlocked the door, exited the bathroom, and closed the door behind him, shutting off the sounds of her heaving.

CHAPTER 26

After a brief detour through the master bedroom bath, where he washed his face in cold water and his hands in antibacterial soap, twice over, Thump found Tiffany in the crowded living room. She was chatting with the HR director, Tecumseh, both of them sipping wine.

Tecumseh grabbed a glass from a passing waiter and handed it to Thump. “Great party,” she said, raising her glass.

“Couldn’t be better.” Thump emptied his glass in a single gulp. “Ah, I needed that.”

Tiffany looked at him. “Are you all right?”

“I’ll be better tomorrow.”

“You’re sweating.” She used a paper napkin to wipe his forehead, then felt it with her hand. “No fever, but you don’t look well. What’s wrong?”

“Office stuff,” he said. “Nothing too serious.”

“Forget the office,” Tecumseh said. “Tonight is about you guys. Have you made wedding plans yet?”

“Not yet,” Tiffany said. “It all happened so quickly, haven’t had time to even think of the wedding. My family is in Tennessee, so they’ll probably want us to get married there. But our life is in Baltimore—work, future, all that—maybe it’s better to have it here.” She looked at Thump. “What do you think?”

“What?” Thump was distracted. “I missed it—”

“Your wedding,” Tecumseh said. “Tennessee or Maryland?”

“Oh.” He smiled. “Here or there, I’ll attend, for sure.”

“You better,” Tiffany said, putting her arm around his waist.

"I'm ready. Are you free tomorrow, lunchtime?"

They laughed.

Through the packed room, Thump caught a glimpse of Henrietta Kingman by the front door, slipping out of the apartment.

Shortly after midnight, the door closed behind the last of the guests. The caterer's cleaning crew was finishing up. Tiffany and Thump stood at the window, watching a brightly lit boat easing out of a nearby marina and gaining speed toward the dark bay.

"It was a lovely party," Tiffany said.

Thump nodded.

"Your colleagues seem nice."

"Ah ha."

She looked at him. "Are you feeling sick or something?"

"I'm fine. Totally fine." He took her hand and kissed it. "A little nervous, that's all. It's the presentation tomorrow. I need it to go perfectly."

Tiffany put her arm around his waist. "I'm sure it will go just fine."

"It has to. Everything depends on it."

Her head rested against his shoulder, and they stood in silence for a few minutes.

"It's getting late," she finally said. "Do you want me to stay over?"

He turned to her, his face lit up. "Are you sure?"

CHAPTER 27

On Friday morning, Thump woke up with Tiffany in his arms, the way they had fallen asleep only a few hours earlier. The mattress rested on the master bedroom floor, right under the windows, now filled with gray clouds.

Tiffany, still half asleep, cuddled closer to him and sighed. He found her lips and kissed her. She reciprocated, opening her eyes. Their bodies responded to each other, their breathing quickened.

Feeling the floor with his hand, Thump found his pants, reached into the pocket, and pulled out a Bull-M condom.

Tiffany saw it, took it from him, and dropped it.

Thump tilted his head in question.

She smiled and showed him her ring finger.

As they made love, raindrops began tapping the window.

Lying on their backs, shoulder to shoulder, panting, Thump and Tiffany looked at each other and smiled.

A phone rang. It was Thump's mobile. He reached over Tiffany and picked it up from the floor. Andy's face was on the screen.

"Happy Friday morning!" Thump lay down on his back. "What's up?"

"It's not here," Andy said. "I can't find it."

"You can't find what?"

"The PowerPoint presentation."

"What are you talking about?" Thump sat up. "It's on my laptop. Open the file—"

"I opened the file. Here, I'll click on it again: *Boulder Trust Board Presentation.* The file opens, but there's no document in it. It's empty!"

"That's impossible." Thump scrambled out of bed. "Search again."

"I've searched again." Andy's voice was filled with panic. "And again, and again."

Pulling on his pants, Thump dropped the phone. Tiffany picked it up and handed it to him, her face worried.

"Andy," he said into the phone, "go down the list of files, see if there's a duplicate."

"I did. Ten times already!"

"Try to reboot my laptop. Sometimes it helps—"

"And it's not on the main server either!"

"I know that," Thump said as he slipped on the shirt he had worn last night. "I didn't save it on the main server."

"You didn't? Why?"

"Because I don't want anybody accessing it. It's my presentation."

"It *was* your presentation," Andy cried. "Now it's gone!"

"Calm down." Thump held the phone with his shoulder while pulling on socks. "It's not gone."

"It is!"

"I'm on my way, OK? We'll find it together." Hanging up, he hurried across the room to the master bathroom.

Tiffany got out of bed, wrapped herself in a sheet, and approached the bathroom. But hearing the sound of him peeing, she changed direction and left the master bedroom.

Entering the hallway bathroom, Tiffany glanced at the mirror and paused, noticing two palm prints, spaced apart. Using the corner of the sheet she was wrapped in, she wiped the mirror clean.

Sitting on the toilet, she saw a discarded Bull-M condom wrapper on the floor by her foot, and then noticed the silk panties on the floor by the wall. She picked up the panties with a hooked pinky and looked closely at the monogram initials.

HDK.

"Tiff?" Thump's voice came from down the hallway. "Where are you?"

She could hear his steps approaching.

He appeared in the doorway, and his eyes dropped to the panties.

Tiffany let go of the panties. Her face twisted in agony. She got up and ran by him and down the hallway to the master bedroom.

Thump stood there, paralyzed, while the sound of her sobbing filled the apartment.

A moment later she reappeared, fully dressed, and hurried by him to the front door. He tried to speak, but no words came out of his mouth.

At the door, Tiffany pulled the engagement ring from her finger and threw it at him. It hit the naked wood floor and skipped a few times before coming to a stop at his feet. Then she was gone.

The homeless man stood under a store canopy and watched through the rain as the convertible Audi sped down Lombard Street, hit the brakes hard, and took the turn to Charles Street fast enough to make the tires slip before recovering traction. The Audi raced up Charles, splashing through deep puddles. At the KKG building, the brake lights came on, and the car swerved left and then turned sharply to the right, stopping hard at the garage entrance, perpendicular across the pavement. After a brief moment, it disappeared inside. The homeless man sighed. He looked up from under the canopy. The morning sky was almost black, letting out rain as thick as a waterfall.

CHAPTER 28

Ruth O'Connor and her husband, Jerald, sipped tea while watching the evening news in their modest living room. Behind them, rain pounded the dark windows.

"The Boulder Charitable Trust," a reporter said, "announced earlier today that its board adopted a new strategic plan to use its substantial principal funds to promote freedom and democracy through investments in socially responsible, virtuous companies."

O'Connor put down her tea. "Clever weasels."

"Board Chairwoman Sharon Boulder noted that the new strategic plan was the brainchild of KKG Investment Management, a prominent Baltimore firm that has managed the Boulder Trust's investments since the late Hank Boulder formed it almost three decades ago. KKG's management contract was renewed today without opposition after a challenger dismissed its attorney, former state judge Ruth O'Connor, who was accused of making racist comments—"

"Liar!" O'Connor grabbed the remote, changed channels, and King Kong appeared, fighting for his life at the top of the Empire State Building. "I wasn't dismissed. I resigned!"

Jerald rose with difficulty and picked up the teacups and saucers. "You've become controversial, dear."

"I'm not a racist. My objections are to their culture of lawlessness, not their skin color."

"That's a lawyerly distinction." He limped to the kitchen. "Nobody can hear logical semantics when they're busy yelling about racism. It's too emotional."

"I've said nothing about race."

"When you criticize a racial group collectively, they'll call you a racist."

"I criticize the blacks of urban ghettos and drug violence, not all blacks." O'Connor got up, went to the window, and watched the rain. "It was humiliating enough to be forced off the bench and back into lawyering, but I did it, I resigned voluntarily to avoid a public scandal. So much for the chief judge's promises of confidentiality."

Jerald rinsed a cup. "This storm shall also pass."

On the TV, King Kong fell to his death.

"They won't let it go," O'Connor said, "until I kneel down and beg forgiveness and say it's commendable to deal drugs, to impregnate schoolgirls—"

"Ruth, please!"

"—to murder each other at random, to suckle at the government's welfare teat shamelessly for five generations—"

Jerald dropped a cup in the sink, and it shattered.

He turned the faucet off and wiped his hands.

"Did you hurt yourself?"

"No," he said. "I'm fine."

"It's overwhelming." Her voice quivered. "My anger, coming back like this, after so many years."

He limped over and hugged her from behind. "Anger is like a dormant volcano, remains boiling hot inside. The thin crust sometimes cracks, that's all."

She wiped her eyes. "My mistake was to say yes to the governor back then, when he nominated me. It was an error. I let vanity cloud my judgment."

"Every lawyer wants to become *Your Honor*. It's natural."

"True." She smiled. "But I should've known better. I should not have become a judge, not in a majority black city. All those cases, one after the other, ugly crimes and black defendants, they got to me, and I couldn't keep my stupid mouth shut."

"Don't beat yourself up." Jerald gently kissed the back of her head. "They would've left you alone if they knew what had happened to you."

"You think?" O'Connor took his hand and held to her cheek. "We'll never know, will we?"

PART II:

Winter

CHAPTER 29

A snowplow rumbled down Pratt Street, clearing a fresh path while snow continued to fall. Following close behind was a taxi, which stopped in front of Chez François. A single passenger came out of the cab, trotted through the snow, and entered the restaurant under the arch of blinking Christmas lights.

Inside it was warm, filled with the patrons' clinking utensils, quiet chatter, and hushed laughter. From ceiling speakers came the soft, clear voice of Charles Aznavour, singing "La Bohème."

The man, who seemed no older than forty, handed his coat and beret to the maître-d' and followed her to the table.

Thump looked up. "Dr. Le Pierre?"

"Mr. Jefferson?" He had a French accent, even more pronounced than on the phone. "I apologize for being late."

"No problem." Thump extended his hand, smiling widely, but didn't get up. "It took us a couple of months to make it happen, so a few more minutes didn't hurt at all."

"Pleasure to meet you."

They shook hands.

"I was in surgery." Dr. Le Pierre sat down. "Then the weather is very bad also." He reached into his breast pocket, pulled out a business card, and handed it over.

"Thank you." Thump put the card by his plate and offered his own card.

A waiter came over and filled their glasses from a half empty wine bottle that was already on the table.

"To mutual prosperity!" Thump raised his glass. "Cheers!"

"Santé!" Dr. Le Pierre took a sip, glancing at Thump's business card.

The waiter set down a small glass bowl before each of them with layered crab meat, avocado, and red grapefruit slices. "Crab verrines," the waiter said. "Bon appétit!"

"Merci," Thump said.

Dr. Le Pierre was still examining the business card. "Are you not with KKG?"

"No longer. It was time for a change. KKG has become too conservative for me, too rigid for this high-technology era, which requires flexibility and speed to take advantage of financial news and investment opportunities."

His fork aimed at the appetizer, Dr. Le Pierre waited for more.

"Jefferson Investments." Thump pointed at his card. "My own investment advisory firm. Unlike KKG, my firm will be nimble, creative, adaptable, tailored to clients' individual investment goals. Here!" He took out a trifold brochure and handed it over. "This is a preliminary version, but it gives you a clear idea of my vision."

Dr. Le Pierre put down his fork and looked at the brochure.

"You tell me," Thump said. "What can I do to earn your business? Go on, challenge me!"

Aznavour gave way to Jacques Brel, who began to sing "Ne Me Quitte Pas."

Dr. Le Pierre put down the trifold. "I don't know. Maybe if I check with KKG, yes? For a reference? Yes?"

Thump leaned forward and took a deep breath. "Look, to be honest, we didn't part ways on the most friendly terms. It was a personality conflict, nothing about money or clients. No irregularity, I assure you. My record is stellar. Absolutely clean."

The music volume was raised, and Brel's voice filled the restaurant. Around them, the patrons were not talking any more, only listening, couples looking at each other, holding hands across the tables.

Glancing over his shoulder, Dr. Le Pierre seemed to seek an escape route.

"I'm not asking for the moon," Thump said, his tone pleading. "Don't transfer all your savings. Give me a chance to manage a portion, to show you what I can do."

"I'm very sorry." Le Pierre got up. "I wish you well."

Thump watched him go.

At the next table, an elderly man reached over and caressed a woman's cheek, repeating after Brel, chanting the French words.

"Excuse me," Thump said. "What does it mean? The lyrics?"

The man, his voice filled with emotions, translated, "Let me be a shadow, your shadow, the shadow of your hand, of your dog … *Ne me quitte pas* … Don't leave me …"

Up front, Dr. Le Pierre collected his coat and hat, glanced back, and left.

"Don't leave me, eh?" Thump picked up the wine bottle and drank directly from it until it was empty. Then he laughed.

Around him, patrons glanced, then looked away.

Regaining his composure, Thump beckoned the waiter and pointed at the appetizers. "Take these away."

The waiter carried the dishes off, crossing paths with Mrs. Jefferson, who was pushing a wheelchair.

Thump dropped a few bills on the table. He shifted sideways in the wooden chair and used both hands to pull his right leg from under the table. His leg was in a cast from ankle to hip.

He unbuttoned his suit jacket, exposing a bulky brace that held his hips and lower back.

Mrs. Jefferson positioned the wheelchair and locked its wheels. She faced Thump, leaned forward, and grasped him by the upper arms. "Ready? On the count of three."

CHAPTER 30

Most of the boats at the marina were covered up for the winter, but the day's moderate temperatures and clear sky attracted a few brave souls. The last snow had mostly melted, leaving white patches in shady areas.

Steady Hands was tied up at the outer dock, where it could easily sail out. Next to it, dwarfed by comparison, was a sharp-looking motorboat, its engine idling. Thump sat on the open deck, bundled up in a winter coat, his cast leg stretched forward. The boat owner, a bearded man in sweat suit and captain's cap, stood at the controls. He glanced at his watch.

A man in a business coat and a scarf walked down the dock, hands deep in his pockets. He looked up at the *Steady Hands.*

"Dr. Jonas?" Thump waved. "Over here!"

The man walked over, still glancing up at the *Steady Hands.*

"I'm T.M. Jefferson." With difficulty, Thump pulled himself up, holding on to the railing. "Come aboard!"

Dr. Jonas stopped at the edge of the dock and gestured at the motorboat. "This isn't the *Steady Hands.*"

The owner laughed. "Obviously!"

"Pleasure to meet you." Thump reached over the side, balancing precariously, and offered his hand. "Come aboard, let's enjoy the nice weather, discuss how I can serve your investment needs—"

"Yes, hi." He shook Thump's hand. "Look, no offense, but I don't know you."

"Of course." Thump handed him a business card. "Here you go."

He looked at the card. “I thought you were with KKG.”

“Our ships parted ways.” Thump held his hands together, then moved them apart. “We follow different stars. It’s the vision thing, you know? Please, join us, and I’ll tell you more about what had—”

“Give me a minute.” Dr. Jonas pulled out his phone, stepped aside, and made a call, speaking in a hushed voice.

The boat owner glanced at Thump while seagulls circled the boat, crowing.

“Hold on,” Dr. Jonas said into his phone as he stepped closer to the boat. “Can you repeat what you just said?” He put the call on speaker and held the phone up.

“Mr. Jefferson no longer works here.” It was Tecumseh’s voice, but instead of her usual joviality, her tone was laconic, as if she was quoting a written statement. “Due to confidentiality laws and the risk of litigation, we cannot provide any further details about the circumstances of Mr. Jefferson’s dismissal from the firm. However, other KKG professionals stand ready to help you with any investment management and advisory services you may require.”

Dr. Jonas hung up and walked away.

The boat owner shrugged and turned off the engine.

CHAPTER 31

After a week of moderate temperatures and clear sky, it had snowed again that morning. O'Connor kept her coat on as she sat in her office, browsing a file of documents brought in by a new client. Seated across the desk, he was a stocky white man with ruddy skin who smelled of cigarette smoke.

"My ex-wife also attended St. Mary's College." He peered at the framed certificates, which Jerald had unpacked and propped up on the credenza. "She went in a junior heifer, came out a fat cow." He laughed.

Glancing at him coldly, O'Connor returned to the documents.

"Look at this one: Yale Law School." He snorted. "Can't wait to tell my buddies I got me a Yale lawyer to sue that stealing SOB."

"I assume you're referring to your former partner, who allegedly stole money from the meat-packing business—"

"What do you mean *allegedly*? He did. It's all in there." He pointed to the file. "Bank statements, checks, receipts, that kinda stuff, how he done it, the fuckin' thief!"

"I'll draft a demand letter—"

"Screw that. I want to sue the bastard."

"It's customary to first send a letter outlining our claims, give the other side a chance to come clean."

"Clean? The guy is dirty, head to toes. You could scrub him with bleach, won't make a difference. You know why? Because his soul is black!"

"I don't think hygiene is our mission here. If you can get your money without litigation, everyone will be better off."

“He won’t fuckin’ pay. We go straight to court. You’re good at that, huh?”

Sitting back, O’Connor said, “If you don’t mind me asking, why did you come to me? There are a million lawyers in this city.”

“A million wimps.” He grinned with yellow teeth.

“How do you know I’m not a wimp like my colleagues?”

“Oh no. Not you. You’re not afraid of them.”

Jerald limped into O’Connor’s office.

“Them?” O’Connor looked at the client. “Who’s them?”

“Them coons, that’s who. You got balls, tellin’ it like it is. How’d you say? Their culture!” He roared in laughter. “Black fuckin’ culture!”

Before O’Connor had time to snap, Jerald pulled the client by the arm. “Come with me, sir. I’ll open the file, take all your information.”

“And take a fuckin’ deposit on our fees,” O’Connor said.

CHAPTER 32

An hour or so later, O'Connor was working at her desk, drafting the complaint over the theft of the meat-packing company's funds. She shook her head and said quietly to herself, "Balls. Damn right I got balls."

A creaking sound came from the door. She looked up and saw a black man rolling into her office in a wheelchair.

"Excuse me!" O'Connor got up. "This is a private office!"

He kept coming toward her desk, his eyes behind sunglasses, a wool cap pulled down to his eyebrows.

She stood and yelled, "Jerald! Jerald!"

"He must have stepped out." The black man removed his sunglasses and smirked.

"Jerald!" O'Connor went around the desk and toward the door.

The black man reached with his left hand and grabbed her arm. "Don't you recognize me?"

"Hey!" She was shouting now. "Let go! Jerald!"

Releasing her arm, he said, "We all look alike to you, don't we?"

Stepping back, panting, O'Connor looked at him, unsure. Only now she noticed that his right leg was in a cast.

"T.M. Jefferson. I was with John Davis at the court hearing about the Boulder Trust a couple of months ago."

Finally O'Connor recognized him. "Oh." She leaned on the credenza for support.

"Are you going to faint?"

"I'm fine." She took a deep breath. "Yes, I remember you now. We were in front of Judge Clarence. You were KKG's fig leaf."

He pulled off the wool cap.

"How are things at the temple of greed?"

"I don't know. They fired me."

"They did?" O'Connor returned to her desk. "And now you want to sue them, right?"

He nodded.

"What for?" She sat down. "Don't answer. Let me guess. Moments after they fired you, as you were walking out the door, you tripped and fell. There's nothing on the X-rays, but you claim to experience a lot of pain, numbness, and inability to walk. Maybe you tore something, or suffered nerve damage. A sympathetic doctor put a cast on your leg, just in case, and now you're in a wheelchair, ready for a million-dollar lawsuit against KKG. Teach them a lesson. Did I guess right?"

Grasping the wheels, he shifted the chair's position, turning toward the door. "I made a mistake coming here."

"Sensitive, are we?" O'Connor knuckled her desk. "Let's start again. Tell me your grievance. I'd like to know."

Thump looked at her. "Are you done insulting me?"

"Yes."

"Then I'll tell you what happened." He shifted in the chair, grunting with pain. "One day after the court hearing, I was promoted to vice president. Also, I conceived a whole new investment strategy for the Boulder Trust. Perhaps you heard about it?"

"Something about buying stock in righteous companies?"

"Virtuous companies."

"That's what it was. Investing in virtuous companies as a way to promote freedom and democracy."

"I came up with it, wrote a whole presentation."

"Clever idea." She sneered. "As credible as the healthy food menu at McDonald's, but it sounds great."

"I like McDonald's." Thump grasped the chair's armrests. "Shall I continue?"

"Go ahead."

"I was supposed to appear before the board of trustees to lay out the whole strategy, show them promising investment targets that I had identified, and guide them through the adoption of the new strategy. But my PowerPoint presentation disappeared from my laptop before the board meeting."

"How convenient. What happened then?"

"Mr. Kolbe told me to keep looking while he went to the board meeting and presented the concept without me. He knew enough to wing it. He's a brilliant man, very personable, charming."

"Did you find the presentation?"

"It was gone. We couldn't recover it. But I heard through the staff that the Boulder Trust's board meeting went well and that they adopted the new strategy based on Mr. Kolbe's explanation. I was incredibly relieved that everything worked out. Later that afternoon, I was summoned to his office for what I expected to be a celebration of our success."

"But it wasn't a celebration." O'Connor leaned forward, curious now. "Tell me what happened."

Thump entered Mr. Kolbe's office. In addition to Mr. Kolbe, he saw Henrietta Kingman, Arthur Goldberg, Bo Chang, and a court stenographer with her machine. All seats were taken.

"Here you are!" Mr. Kolbe beckoned him. "Come on in, join us."

Thump looked for a place to sit, but there was none. "I heard the good news," he said. "They adopted our proposed strategy."

"It wasn't easy," Mr. Kolbe said.

"I'm terribly sorry about the presentation. I don't understand how it vanished."

"How?" Kingman didn't look at him. "That's immaterial. Clients judge investment managers on results, not on excuses."

"It's not an excuse." Thump was shocked by her hostility. "It's a fact."

"Look," Mr. Kolbe said, "mistakes happen. This firm prides itself on nurturing excellence in our employees, helping them maximize their potential, learn from their mistakes. Sure. But an error of this magnitude? I don't know how we can overlook it."

"I worked all week," Thump said. "It was a great presentation!"

"Was it?" Kingman chuckled humorlessly. "We only saw a half-baked draft on Wednesday, and that draft was missing a lot of numbers."

"But I finished it later. All the numbers were in, even the logo of each of the companies we recommended, as Mrs. Boulder had suggested. But someone went into my office, turned on my laptop, and deleted—"

"Someone else," Kingman said. "Not you. You're the victim, right?"

"It's not my fault that the presentation was deleted—"

"Get real, Thump," Goldberg said. "You didn't even save a backup copy on the main server. We almost lost our biggest account!"

"And that," Chang said, "would have killed our chance of winning the Teachers' Pension Fund contract."

Looking at the half circle of unsmiling faces, Thump raised his hands defensively. "I know how it looks, but I have never lost a document before. Never!"

"This," Mr. Kolbe said, "was more than a document. It was our sales pitch to the Boulder Trust, our concept for the future of the relationship. It was our raison d'être."

Everyone nodded.

"Let me tell you," Mr. Kolbe said. "I had to use all my schmoozing skills. I had to improvise and deliver a convincing strategic presentation on the fly, with no data, no examples, no statistical analysis, or verifiable projections. My personal reputation suffered, and our firm's reputation was dented. Mr. Jefferson, I must say, you put us in a terrible position!"

The stenographer kept typing fast.

"We're lucky," Kingman said, "that Sharon Boulder managed to sugarcoat the situation, soft-pedal the whole thing to the trustees."

Realizing he had no chance to justify his failure, Thump pressed a contrite hand to his chest. "From the bottom of my heart, I apologize. And I give you my word: it will never happen again."

"You're damn right," Kingman said. "It won't happen again."

Mr. Kolbe gestured to calm her and smiled at Thump. "Young man, please understand one thing. This hurts us more than it hurts you. But we're confident that a person of your personal charm and capabilities will have no problem finding a new—"

"Wait a minute." Thump was incredulous. "Are you firing me?"

In O'Connor office, Thump's fist pounded the wheelchair's armrest. "It was a setup! Someone deleted the file from my laptop, and that gave them an excuse to fire me!"

"That's a serious accusation," she said. "Can you prove it?"

He shook his head.

"Were you in a wheelchair when all this happened?"

"Not yet, but later, on the same—"

"Then it's irrelevant," O'Connor said. "Why don't you move on, get a new job?"

"You think I haven't tried?" Thump struggled to control his anger. "My only credential is having worked at KKG. Being dismissed without a letter of reference is like a professional execution. Nobody will hire me, and no client will do business with me."

"Sad stories don't make legal cases. To file a court action, you need evidence that they broke the law. But from what you're describing, they had a valid cause to fire you."

"What if they had a different motive?"

"Like what?"

"Sexual harassment."

O'Connor raised her eyebrows. "I see. They fired you after falsely—" She signaled quotation marks with her hands. "—falsely accusing you of sexually harassing a woman at the office. Is that what you're claiming?"

Thump chuckled sadly, shaking his head. "Do you work hard at being a devil's advocate, or does it come naturally to you?"

"It comes naturally. Who did they accuse you of harassing? Your secretary?"

"They didn't accuse me of harassing anybody. It's the other way around. I was the victim of sexual harassment."

O'Connor grinned. "You? That's a first."

"It's the truth."

"Who abused you?"

"Henrietta Kingman. Also with her clients, rich widows, business women she wanted to—"

"Kingman? That shrimpy redhead and her lady friends forced a strapping VP, a body-building Casanova, to do it with them?"

"It's not about physical size. And I did go along with it for a long time, but eventually I refused. She forced me to do it, and when I wouldn't, she made me go down—"

"That's enough." O'Connor raised a hand. "Let's skip the details right now. Even if this really happened, you first have to file a complaint with the Equal Employment Opportunity Commission. Have you?"

"Yes. They declined to take action, said there's no corroborative evidence, and that it seems like I was fired for a valid cause. But I can still sue KKG in court, right?"

"Theoretically you can sue anybody in court. The question is what are your chances of winning. How many lawyers have you amused with this novelty case?"

"Six."

"Now it's seven." O'Connor stood. "There's no valid legal claim here. But it's an original story. You could pitch this plotline to movie producers: Jessica Lange being sued for sexually harassing King Kong."

Thump turned his wheelchair and rolled toward the door. "I'm not an ape," he said.

Thump pushed out through the front door of the building and rolled the wheelchair down the sidewalk as fast as he could. Mrs. Jefferson came out of an old minivan and, seeing him fly like this, signaled him to slow down. But she was too late, and the wheelchair caught on a snow bank and tipped over, throwing Thump into the muddy slush. He shouted in frustration, hitting the ground with his hands.

CHAPTER 33

Leaving downtown Baltimore, Mrs. Jefferson drove onto the 395 Freeway, past the Ravens ballpark and over the water, when Thump suddenly yelled from the back:

"Stop! Stop! Stop!"

She veered to the shoulder and stopped.

Thump grabbed the handle and slid open the door. He slipped off the tied-up wheelchair down onto the floor of the minivan and scooted out the door. Pulling himself up, he managed to stand on his left leg, holding on to the minivan.

His mother ran around the front and tried to hold him, but Thump twisted away from her and fell forward to the iron railing, dragging his casted leg behind. Far below, the murky water of a Chesapeake Bay estuary rippled in the light wind.

"This isn't a good place to stop." She glanced at the cars and trucks rushing by, tires rattling on the uneven concrete. "We need to go."

"You can go," he yelled over the noise. "Leave me here!"

"Don't be ridiculous."

"Go! Please go!" He swayed, but held on to the hip-high railing. "I'm done. That's it for me."

"That's it?" She placed her hands on her hips. "You're giving up?"

He looked at the water, not responding.

"What right do you have to give up?" She shook a finger at him. "Answer me, Thurgood Marshall Jefferson! Is this life yours to give up?"

He lowered his head.

"Is this what I worked for all these years, breaking my back so you could stand straight? Stand tall? Did I raise you to give up?"

Thump gestured her to leave.

"Alright. I'm leaving. You want to be done with it all? Is that it?"

He nodded.

"Then I'm done wasting my life trying to make a man out of you." Mrs. Jefferson started for the car, but paused. "Don't you love Tiffany anymore?"

He glanced at his mother, then looked down at the water again. "I think of her all the time." He choked up. "Far as she's concerned, I'm the bad guy."

"Are you?"

"I did bad things, ugly things, made stupid decisions. It's all true. I did bad, Mamma, but I'm not a bad person." He paused, fighting off tears. "I had to do these things. They left me no choice."

"Then you should stop whining and stand up for yourself. Fight!"

"How? You should have heard what the lawyer said. I have no case against them."

"What lawyer? That white judge? The racist one?"

"Who knows the law better than a judge?"

"God knows the law better than all the judges. And the good Lord knows what's in your heart. Now, answer my question: Was it your fault?"

"I don't know anymore."

"Then make up your mind, son, because no one will believe in you until you believe in yourself."

A lull in traffic brought a temporary quietness.

"It doesn't matter," he said. "Tiffany will never believe."

"Maybe. Maybe not," Mrs. Jefferson said. "But if you don't fight for the truth to come out, for your redemption, you won't find out."

A gap opened in the clouds above, and the sun shone through. Thump craned his head and looked up at the sky, squinting his eyes.

CHAPTER 34

At the Baltimore Aquatic Center, O'Connor sat in an open veranda and watched the group of disabled men exercising in the pool. The group was mixed—whites, blacks, and a few Hispanics and Asians—with several physical therapists in orange swim caps wading from one patient to another.

Jerald waved from the pool, and she waved back. A black man also waved. It took her a moment to recognize him. It was Thump. She waved back at him. A woman in hospital scrubs, sitting nearby, also waved.

"Hi," the woman said. She was heavyset, her hair turning silver, her smile wide and bright like Thump's. "Do you know my son?"

"We've met. I'm Ruth O'Connor."

Mrs. Jefferson's smile faded away. She resumed reading through papers she had in her lap.

The disabled men slipped on colorful flotation rings and started playing ball. They looked like kids, and there was a lot of laughter.

O'Connor noticed Mrs. Jefferson's papers were court decisions. "Is he pursuing the case pro se?"

"Excuse me?"

"Pro se. It means representing himself, going to court without legal counsel."

"That's right." Mrs. Jefferson returned to reading.

"I would have taken the case if I thought he had a chance."

"You mean, if he had white skin?"

"No," O'Connor said, "I mean what I say. And I don't care about my clients' skin color. I care about the law. KKG fired him for a reason—"

"For the wrong reason!" Mrs. Jefferson glared at her.

"Look, I understand your anger. He's your son, and he's hurting. Losing a job is terrible. I know it. But if you made a fatal mistake at the hospital, wouldn't they fire you?"

"Refusing sex with the boss is a mistake?"

O'Connor considered the question for a moment. "When sex goes on for a long time without complaining, it creates an assumption that it's consensual."

"That's nonsense. If all the facts were the same, except that he wasn't a young black man but a beautiful white girl who had to sleep with an older partner to succeed at her career, you'd take this case like this!" Mrs. Jefferson snapped her fingers. "No question about it."

"Maybe." O'Connor reflected on it for a moment. "You mentioned that he refused. What happened to make him suddenly refuse?"

"To keep his vow to his fiancée."

"He didn't tell me about that." O'Connor looked at Thump, who caught the ball in the pool and passed it in a perfectly aimed throw to another man. "Are they still engaged?"

Mrs. Jefferson shook her head. "That's the real reason he wants to sue them. He's determined to prove in court that they forced him to do all those things. It's his only chance to try and win her forgiveness." She watched Thump in the pool. "He's a good son."

After a long moment, O'Connor said, "We couldn't have children."

"Your husband seems much older than you."

"He is, but it wasn't his fault. I couldn't carry a pregnancy."

There was a long pause before O'Connor explained.

"While in college, I was attacked. They really messed me up—"

Mrs. Jefferson inhaled and pressed a hand to her chest.

"Jerald and I met much later. I was a prosecutor already. He was a character witness in a sentencing hearing for one of his high school students. The kid robbed three 7-Eleven stores in one night. Jerald testified about how the defendant was a good student, how his family circumstances left him no choice, and so on. I ripped into Jerald, but he remained calm and pleasant as if we were chatting at Starbucks. Couple of weeks later he called the office and asked me out. We married, and for a while we considered adopting, but our work consumed us, and we found fulfillment in other ways."

"The Lord give us what he thinks we can handle."

"You think? I sometime question his decisions. Especially back in college. God must have hated me silly."

"You have some hate in you also."

"It's not hate."

"Sure sounded like hate when you said those things about our people."

O'Connor hesitated. "No, there's no hate. Fear, that's what it is. I fear black men. I can't control it. It's physical, like a phobia, like fear of heights. I've never told this to anyone, but it's true."

"Your secret is safe with me." Mrs. Jefferson reached over and touched her hand. "And you don't need to be afraid of my son."

They watched the men being helped out of the pool—Thump into his wheelchair, his cast wrapped in plastic, and Jerald hopping to a bench on his right leg, his left leg amputated below the knee.

O'Connor pointed. "My husband the skipper."

Mrs. Jefferson laughed.

"He taught high school for thirty-eight years. History and government. Everything for his students, never took care of himself. His diabetes wasn't controlled, took his leg."

"He seems very nice."

"He is nice—for a man."

They shared a chuckle.

O'Connor gestured at the papers. "Would you mind if I looked at these?"

"Be my guest." Mrs. Jefferson handed her the whole pile of court decisions. "It's all Chinese to me."

Jerald drove while O'Connor, in the passenger seat with the pile of papers in her lap, read through the court decisions.

Glancing at the papers, Jerald said, "He did his own research?"

"Pretty much. He went to the office of the legal department at the hospital where his mom works and asked them to help him."

"Good cases?"

"All the relevant decisions are here." She held up the one she was reading. "*Meritor v. Vinson,* the first Supreme Court case to recognize sexual harassment as unlawful discrimination, including 'quid pro quo' relationships and the concept of 'hostile work environment.' And this one," she picked another, "*Harris v. Forklift,* ruled that it's enough to prove that harassment affected an employee's performance or advancement." She flipped through the pile. "Next, *Faragher v. Boca* made corporate employers liable for sexual harassment by supervisors. And *Oncale v. Sundowner* recognized that men could also be victims of sexual harassment."

Slowing down, Jerald turned into their driveway. "So the law is on his side?"

O'Connor watched the garage door open. "Theoretically, if they did what he says, it could be sexual harassment. They'll have a hard time explaining why they terminated his employment soon after he started refusing to engage in sex. But there's a cap on damages for such claims, so lawyers decline to take the cases even when the evidence is favorable, which is questionable in this case."

Jerald maneuvered the car into the garage. "Does he have any other claim?"

"Funny you should ask." O'Connor looked at the next court decision. "He found the right case: plaintiffs in sex discrimination cases may add a cause of action for intentional infliction of emotional distress, for which damage awards are not limited by law."

Turning off the car, Jerald said, "What's your gut feeling about his case?"

"The law is not complicated. It's the facts I'm not sure about." O'Connor unbuckled her seat belt. "His dispute with them will be over the facts, which means he can get a jury trial. But KKG will deny everything. They'll fight hard and dirty."

"Rich jerks. Someone should do it."

"It?"

Jerald stuck up his middle finger. "Thump them!"

They looked at each other and laughed.

CHAPTER 35

Symphony hall erupted in enthusiastic clapping as the orchestra concluded a dramatic finale and the curtain dropped for the intermission. Audience members began to rise from their seats, each row draining slowly into the aisles for the obligatory drinks and restroom visits.

The four KKG partners, however, did not have to shuffle up the aisles or wait in line for refreshments or bladder relief. While most audience members had not yet gotten very far from their seats, Mr. Kolbe, Henrietta Kingman, Arthur Goldberg, and Bo Chang were already sipping wine and nibbling on miniature sandwiches at the firm's private booth, high above the main auditorium.

As a waiter was leaving with an empty tray, O'Connor slipped in through the open door. "Mr. Kolbe," she said. "I'm Ruth O'Connor."

It took him a brief moment to recover, but Mr. Kolbe smiled graciously, shaking her hand. "Of course. How nice to meet you." He gestured at the refreshments. "Would you care for a drink or something to eat?"

"Thank you, but this is not a social call." She handed him a brown envelope. "Here we go. You've been served in your capacity as chairman of KKG Investment Management Inc."

He looked at the envelope as if she had given him a dead rat.

Turning to leave, O'Connor waved her hand toward the stage. "Enjoy. I hear the allegro is to die for!"

They huddled around Mr. Kolbe, reading the complaint together, until he had read enough and shoved the papers back into the envelope.

"Disgusting!" Mr. Kolbe raised the envelope, shaking it. "Filth!"

"It's all lies," Kingman said. "From beginning to end, total fabrication."

"You realize," Goldberg said, "that Thump intentionally hired O'Connor to attract media attention to his lawsuit. What could be more juicy than an infamous racist former judge taking on a sexual harassment case of a black guy against a bunch of white fat cats."

"Ungrateful bastard." Mr. Kolbe emptied a shot of whiskey. "After all we've done for him, he wants to drag us into court in front of the whole business community!"

"Thump is a businessman," Goldberg said. "He's doing this to apply pressure, that's all. It's a settlement he's after, a nice check, not an ugly, prolonged legal battle."

"Might be cheaper," Chang said, "to hold our noses and settle with him right now than pay John Davis huge legal fees while this whole thing plays out in public."

They stayed quiet as a waiter entered, cleared the dishes, and left.

Below, the auditorium darkened and a few musical instruments began tuning.

"No settlement!" Mr. Kolbe sat down and dropped the envelope down on the carpet by his shoes. "He has already filed it. The case is out in public. If we pay him, it will be an admission of guilt. Everyone will assume that we did something wrong. We have to fight back, show that we fired him for incompetence. Our clients expect us to maintain the highest standards!"

Goldberg sat down. "Salacious accusations can stick, even if they're false. A quick settlement and dismissal of the lawsuit—"

"Damn it, Arthur!" Mr. Kolbe glared at him. "Do you know anything about that boy screwing around?"

"No," Goldberg said. "Not really."

CHAPTER 36

Mrs. Jefferson placed loaded dinner plates before Thump and Tiffany, then brought her own plate from the kitchen and sat down. She reached to both of them, and they held her hands. But when Thump tried to hold Tiffany's hand, she moved it away.

"Thank you, Lord," Mrs. Jefferson said, "for the plentiful meal we are about to eat, for the company of those we love, for good health, as well as for healing physical wounds to the body and easing hurtful injuries to the soul. We thank you for your divine presence in our lives, for your blessing and protection, for your infinite wisdom, compassion, understanding, and forgiveness, which are the virtues we aspire to follow in our humble, human, mortal lives, and we say amen."

"Amen," Tiffany said.

Thump sighed, shifted his wheelchair's position slightly, and said, "Amen."

"Enjoy," Mrs. Jefferson said, and they started eating.

The room was decorated with knickknacks and family photos featuring Thump as a baby and as a schoolboy. There he was, playing in little league, then high school track and football, followed by a series of graduation portraits—middle school, high school, and college. Above the mantle was a large oil painting of Dr. Martin Luther King Jr., depicted as he spoke from the podium at the National Mall.

Tiffany was the first to break the silence. "The food is delicious," she said. "Thank you."

Mrs. Jefferson smiled. "Thank you for coming, sweetheart. And for eating. We'll need our strength this week."

Thump put down his fork. "I don't think you should come to court, Mom. You know what this case is about, the stuff that's going to come up—"

"I know what it's about," Mrs. Jefferson said. "And I know where I should be when my son's fighting to prove his innocence."

Tiffany cleared her throat.

"I'm not innocent," Thump said. "The choices I made were wrong. Totally wrong." He glanced at Tiffany. "But KKG, my bosses, they were wrong to force me to choose between success and—"

Tiffany's fork fell from her hand onto her plate.

"Right." Mrs. Jefferson looked up at the oil portrait on the wall. "As the Reverend Dr. King said: '*Every step toward the goal of justice requires sacrifice, suffering, and struggle.*'"

PART III:

Spring

CHAPTER 37

In his courtroom on the seventh floor at the Edward A. Garmatz U.S. Courthouse, Judge Clarence leaned back in his large chair and listened as plaintiff's counsel, Ruth O'Connor, was delivering her opening statement.

The jurors were a mix of ages and genders. An Asian woman of indeterminable age sat next to two African American women—one very heavy, about twenty-five, the other quite elderly with big glasses, her white hair curled up. Next to them was a young black man in a suit, then an old redneck with oily hair and a beer belly, and a young white woman with colorful tattoos and spiky purple hair.

Thump, in his wheelchair, sat alone at the plaintiff's table and watched O'Connor.

"We will show you," she said to the jurors, "that plaintiff T.M. Jefferson was being used, abused, and sexually harassed by his superiors."

She pointed at the defense table, where John W. Davis sat with his associate, Erica Dropper, as well as Mr. Kolbe, Henrietta Kingman, Arthur Goldberg, and Bo Chang.

"They used Mr. Jefferson cynically, forcing him to engage in sexual acts for their personal pleasure, as well as with KKG clients for business development purposes. And when he became engaged and refused to continue, they fired him and caused him physical injuries. Worse yet, by refusing to provide him with a letter of reference, they destroyed his career, deprived him of future employment, and inflicted on him severe emotional distress."

She pointed again. "They will try to confuse and manipulate your sympathies by throwing dirt at their victim. I'm confident nothing will distract you from the truth."

Among the audience, Tiffany was seated next to Mrs. Jefferson, who nodded at the last statement.

John W. Davis stood, buttoned his suit jacket, and looked at Judge Clarence, who gestured his permission to proceed.

Shaking his head, Davis approached the jury box. "This case," he said, "proves a sad yet often true proverb: that no good deed goes unpunished."

He paused to let his declaration—the theme of his defense—sink in, then he gestured at the KKG partners. "Here's a group of dedicated professionals, known for their high integrity and impeccable sense of honor. Clients trust them with large financial investments. They serve the community in important charity, art, and educational causes. And in line with their deep sense of social responsibility, five years ago they hired an inner city kid who got into business school on affirmative action but couldn't even manage to complete the MBA program."

Davis stepped closer to Thump.

"They gave this young man an opportunity that many others could only dream of. They showered him with benefits. They handed to him all the tools he would need to succeed." Davis sighed. "But he failed. And rather than admit his errors and find another job, rather than work hard like the rest of us, rather than taking responsibility for his own failure as an honorable man would do, he came here, to this courtroom, to bite the hands that fed him!"

The audience murmured, but Davis didn't wait.

"Members of the jury," he said. "I submit to you that justice requires total rejection of this R-rated slander. The facts, I am certain, will lead you to the same conclusion so that you will render judgment for KKG."

The jurors' faces reflected their confusion as they watched Davis return to his seat.

“Thank you, Counselors,” Judge Clarence said. “Plaintiff, call your first witness.”

O’Connor stood and said, “I call Henrietta Kingman to the stand.”

CHAPTER 38

The courtroom deputy administered the oath to Kingman, who was dressed in a sand-colored business suit, wore minimal makeup, and had her red hair pulled back in a businesslike tight bun.

"Miss Kingman," O'Connor said, "what's your position at KKG?"

"Second," Kingman said and coughed to clear her voice.

"Excuse me?"

"Second." Kingman looked at the jury box. "I'm the second K in KKG."

The jurors laughed, liking her already.

O'Connor didn't smile. "Please describe your job history at KKG."

"Oh, that's like asking me to describe my whole life," Kingman said. "Well, I started twenty-seven years ago as Mr. Kolbe's secretary. It was a small firm then, and I had to be a jack-of-all-trades. Over the years, I finished my bachelor's degree, got a master's in economics, and earned an MBA while working full time and learning everything I could about the firm's business and about investment management."

The old redneck juror looked at his fellow jurors, his face contorted to show how impressed he was.

"You must be proud of your achievements," O'Connor said.

"I believe in working hard to achieve your goals."

"When did you become a partner?"

"That's easy." Kingman again cleared her throat, which didn't seem to reduce her hoarseness much. "On July fourth, seven years ago, Mr. Kolbe announced it at the company's annual picnic, just before the fireworks." She glanced at Mr. Kolbe, and he looked down.

Seeing this, O'Connor paused for a moment. "Interesting. Now how did you meet Mr. Jefferson?"

"Let's see." Kingman took a moment to remember. "About five years ago, I believe. It was at a lecture I gave to members of the chambers of commerce about opportunities for women and minorities in our industry. It's a subject that's very close to my heart, as you can imagine."

"Did Mr. Jefferson attend the lecture?"

"I don't know. It was a large crowd. But he was there at the end. He came over and handed me his résumé. We chatted, and I was impressed with him."

"Why?"

"He was a very charming young man, well spoken, bursting with energy and ambition. Back in the office, I gave his résumé to our HR department, and they invited him for interviews."

"Was it relevant that he's black?"

"Yes," Kingman said without hesitation. "It was a plus."

"A plus?"

"For legal and business reasons, as our firm has grown in size and prominence, we've tried to diversify our staff."

"Did he fit your hiring criteria?"

"Mr. Jefferson's MBA grades weren't great. In fact, he twice failed one of the required courses. He assured us that he was going to graduate, but I don't think he ever did get his MBA degree."

"Why did you hire someone with a poor academic record?"

"When a candidate shows great promise, you sometimes take a chance. We hoped he'd work hard, meet expectations."

"How did it work out?"

"At first, he met our expectations, even more than that. But as time went on, his attitude and performance deteriorated."

"Didn't KKG promote him repeatedly, every single year, over and over again?"

"I don't know exactly. His employment records—"

"I've reviewed those records." O'Connor read from her notes. "During his five years at the firm, Mr. Jefferson held these successive job titles: Assistant Analyst, Analyst, Senior Analyst, Associate, Senior Associate, and Vice President—the last promotion occurring only one week before you fired him, correct?"

Kingman took a deep breath. "Yes, but let me explain something about our business, which is slightly different from other industries. In the investment management firm environment, the type of work done by professionals does not change materially over the years of seniority. We gain experience as we serve our clients, analyze the markets, identify good investment opportunities, and so on. Therefore, annual promotions are almost automatic. They mean very little."

"But a promotion to vice president," O'Connor said, "an executive-level rank, followed by job termination so soon afterward? Wasn't it odd, even for your unique industry?"

"It hurts me to say this." Kingman paused, her expression reflecting pain. "But Mr. Jefferson completely botched a crucial assignment, failed to deliver a key presentation, and caused a great deal of embarrassment for KKG."

"Was it the Boulder Trust situation?"

"Exactly. In our business, when we handle a large charitable trust, we take extra care to assist the client's board of trustees because they are volunteers. In the case of the Boulder Trust, which is one of the largest in Maryland, the trustees are very busy business executives who volunteer their time. Because of Mr. Jefferson's grave error, they arrived for the annual meeting only to find out at the last minute that we did not have the promised strategy presentation to show them." Kingman looked at the jurors. "We had no choice. We had to fire him."

"But here he is," O'Connor said, "suing you. Why?"

"He is angry. It's human, but unjustified in this case."

"Have you—"

Kingman raised her hand to indicate she wasn't done answering the question. "You know what? If it were me, if I had failed to deliver a major presentation at the last minute, if I had been the one to damage KKG's reputation like this, then I would not have waited to be fired. I would have resigned!"

The jurors looked at each other, clearly impressed.

"This begs the question," O'Connor said, "have you ever considered resigning?"

"No."

"Never crossed your mind to resign from KKG?"

"No." Kingman sat up straight, proud. "KKG Investment Management is my life."

"That's very nice, but you were saying how an error should prompt voluntary resignation. Based on that logic, if you had made a mistake, you should have resigned, correct?"

"Yes."

"Have you not made any mistakes in twenty-seven years? Not even one?"

There was silence in the courtroom, everyone watching Kingman, who seemed to realize how the question had no good answer.

"People make mistakes." Kingman shrugged. "I'm human and I make mistakes. But not of this magnitude."

"Of a lesser magnitude?"

"It happens."

"Can you share one mistake you've made?"

"I don't recall, not right now."

"Not a single mistake?" O'Connor waited. "Let me help you. Was it not a mistake to hire him?" She pointed at Thump.

"In retrospect, yes, it was."

"And since you brought him in, aren't you responsible for his subsequent mistake, which you said justified his termination?"

Some in the audience laughed, but Thump didn't, and after keeping eye contact with Kingman, he lowered his gaze.

"Hiring him wasn't my decision alone," Kingman said. "At least six professionals have to interview a candidate and recommend hiring him. But if I alone were responsible, I would have offered my resignation over the serious mistake of hiring Mr. Jefferson."

"Mr. Jefferson? Is this how you addressed him during the five years he had been working for you—Mr. Jefferson?"

"Everyone called him Thump. He encouraged it, even put it on his vanity license plate."

"Everyone called him Thump," O'Connor repeated. "And on that Friday, when you fired Thump, what happened down on the street between you and Thump?"

Taking a deep breath, Kingman wore a sad expression. "I was driving out of the garage. He was out on the sidewalk, I'm not sure why. He saw me and blocked my way."

"What did you do?"

"Naturally I stepped out of the car to speak with him. He was very upset, begged to be hired back. It was heartbreaking, really, but what could I do? I told him it's not possible, that it's out of my hands."

"What happened then?"

Kingman took her time to answer. "He yelled at me: '*What kind of a monster are you?*' I didn't answer. I saw that he was too upset. But he wouldn't let me go back to my car."

"What type of a car do you drive?"

"It's a small, sporty car," Kingman said.

"What kind?"

"A seven-year-old Ferrari. I bought it after I became a partner. A rare splurge, for me."

"Did he physically stop you from returning to your car? Did he touch you?"

"No. He walked backward, facing me, yelling really loudly."

"Was the street quiet at the time?"

"No, there was a lot of traffic going by, busses and cars."

"So he could have been yelling to overcome the noise, not necessarily out of anger?"

"I don't know," Kingman said. "He seemed to be in a rage, which I think was the reason he didn't pay attention, tripped on the edge of the curb, and fell backward into traffic."

"Was he hit?"

"Yes. A speeding van gave him a glancing blow, shot him back toward the sidewalk, and he fell hard against a fire hydrant." Kingman shut her eyes as if the image was too painful to recall. "The van kept going with the traffic. I don't know if the driver even noticed."

"Did you call for help?"

"There was a homeless man there. He ran over and attended to Mr. Jefferson."

"A homeless man?"

"Yes. He's a regular. I've seen him on the street for years."

"And you?"

"I left."

"In your Ferrari?"

"Yes."

"Let me get this straight." O'Connor looked at her. "You got into your Ferrari and drove off while a man who had worked for you for five years, a man you had fired an hour earlier, was lying on the sidewalk, badly injured?"

"I didn't know he was badly injured."

"Excuse me." O'Connor turned to Judge Clarence. "I'd like to request that the court reporter read back the answer given by the witness after I asked her: 'Was he hit?'"

The judge nodded at the court reporter, who searched her notes and said, "Here, the witness answered as follows: '*Yes. A speeding van gave him a glancing blow, shot him back toward the sidewalk, and he fell hard against a fire hydrant. The van kept going with the traffic, I don't know if the driver even noticed.*'"

"Thank you," O'Connor said, turning back to Kingman. "Wasn't it obvious to you that Mr. Jefferson was badly hurt?"

"It all happened very fast. All I could think about was getting away. He'd been very agitated." Kingman's hoarse voice shook. "I was afraid of him."

The old redneck juror and the white tattooed woman looked at each other.

"When you say that you were afraid of him, do you mean that you feared for your safety, that you feared that Mr. Jefferson would attack you physically?"

"Yes."

"Tell me," O'Connor said. "In five years of working at KKG, has Mr. Jefferson ever attacked anyone?"

"Not to my knowledge."

"Threatened anyone?"

"I don't—" She cleared her throat. "I don't recall."

"Miss Kingman, why are you so hoarse?"

Davis rose to his feet. "Objection! Irrelevant!"

Judge Clarence looked at O'Connor, waiting for an explanation, but she was busy watching Kingman, who glanced at Mr. Kolbe quickly before both of them looked away.

O'Connor turned to the judge. "I withdraw the question."

Davis sat down, satisfied.

"Now, here is a simple question on a different subject." O'Connor stepped closer to the witness stand. "How often did you and Mr. Jefferson have sex?"

"Objection," Davis yelled even before he stood up. "Speculative and vague!"

"Your Honor," O'Connor said to the judge, "this is a sexual harassment case, and the complaint alleges a relationship between them. The question is relevant."

Judge Clarence made a doubtful face. "Objection sustained as to the form of the question. Please rephrase the question specifically to the definition of sexual harassment."

O'Connor glanced at a textbook. "Have you ever pressured Mr. Jefferson to have sex with you or with others?"

Kingman waited to see if Davis would object, but he didn't. "No," she said. "I have not pressured him."

CHAPTER 39

After a ten-minute break, Judge Clarence was back on the bench. Kingman returned to the witness stand, and Davis rose for the cross-examination.

"Could you tell us please," he said, "how did KKG treat the plaintiff?"

Kingman cleared her throat before answering. "We gave him everything to help him achieve success."

"For example?"

"We paid for a wardrobe of tailored suits and monogrammed shirts. We gave him a nice office, fully equipped, as well as a laptop computer, a competent assistant, regular training and professional conferences, a generous expense account to take clients out for meals and entertainment. He had access to our firm's golf membership at the Chesapeake Greens Country Club, where he regularly took potential clients to play, and he had free use of the company yacht, the *Steady Hands*, with crew and a fully staffed kitchen—she's a favorite among our clients."

"Did he show gratitude for this generosity?"

"At first he did. But as time went on, his attitude became troubling."

"In what way?"

Kingman reflected on the question before answering. "He avoided clients' calls, telling his assistant to take messages, which often remained unreturned. He left the office during working hours for—according to office gossip—romantic trysts with various women. He gave reckless advice to clients, slacking on research and on prudence, which KKG prides itself on."

"Of course," Davis said. "And how was his relationship with colleagues?"

"He often disrupted other employees' work, spending hours at the office kitchenette, regaling the staff with stories, some of them off-colored."

"But you kept him on. Why?"

"Look, at KKG, when we hire someone, we make a long-term commitment of total support, all out, so he'll succeed." She looked at Thump. "Even when all the signs indicate that this wasn't a good fit, we're reluctant to give up on a colleague. It's truly devastating when there's such total letdown. It's not only the person who leaves. It's also our failure as a team."

At the defense table, Mr. Kolbe nodded gravely.

CHAPTER 40

As soon as the judge broke for lunch, Thump raced in his wheelchair out of the courtroom, down the hallway, to the men's room. He was having a severe attack of stomach cramps, and time was running out.

The last stall, made wide for wheelchair access, was free. Maneuvering inside, he groaned with pain. As soon as the cramp eased, he struggled to get up, his weight on the left leg, but he forgot to lock the wheels, and the chair sprang out from under him. He tried to hold onto the door, but lost his balance and fell.

John W. Davis, with Mr. Kolbe and Arthur Goldberg, entered the men's room. "My rebuttal," Davis was saying, "will drive a deadly spear through the soft belly of their circumstantial evidence—"

They noticed Thump on the floor, his head sticking out from the last stall, facing them.

"Oh my God!" Goldberg started forward, but Mr. Kolbe grabbed his arm.

Davis turned. "I'll call the court deputy."

Goldberg shook free of Mr. Kolbe's grasp and went to help Thump.

Mr. Kolbe grunted and left.

"Here, I'll hold you under your arms." Goldberg supported Thump as he stood up and gripped the handicap railing.

"Thank you." Thump used one hand to unbuckle his belt. "You better leave quickly. I'm about to explode."

Goldberg stepped back and closed the door.

CHAPTER 41

O'Connor called Tim Cox as her second witness. He was a smallish white man, about thirty, with jittery hands, a toothy grin, and a dark-green suit with a mismatched blue tie.

"Mr. Cox," O'Connor said, "do you recognize one of your MBA classmates in this courtroom?"

"I certainly do. Thurgood Marshall Jefferson, right over there." He winked at Thump. "How you doin', big guy?"

"The witness," Judge Clarence said, "will answer counsel's questions and refrain from extraneous communications or direct interactions with others during his testimony."

"Sorry." Cox saluted the judge.

O'Connor swallowed her smile. "Did you know him as Mr. Jefferson?"

"We called him Thump."

"Do you recall how Mr. Jefferson got a job at KKG?"

"Sure I do. He owed it to me."

"How so?"

"I found out that Henrietta Kingman was going to speak at the COC event. We printed our CVs and went there. After the lecture, we went up to her and introduced ourselves."

"How did it go?"

"She had eyes only for him."

Murmurs passed through the audience in the courtroom.

"And you," O'Connor asked, "did she speak with you at all?"

"It wasn't easy. They were chatting on as if I didn't exist. I nudged him and said, 'Hey, Thump, would you like me to bring you two something to drink? A few pretzels maybe?' So she laughed, sent him to fetch us drinks, and I was happy to have a chance to talk with Henrietta Kingman alone. I had a whole pitch memorized about how I'd fit perfectly at KKG."

"Did you deliver it?"

"No. She wanted to talk about something else."

"About what?"

"About Thump."

Now the audience laughed loudly.

"What about him?"

"She asked why he's nicknamed Thump."

"What was your answer?"

"I told her that the guys call him Thump because it's the sound of him entering the locker room showers, his thing hitting the floor, *Thump! Thump! Thump*!"

The audience laughed harder, and Judge Clarence hit the gavel.

When the courtroom quieted down, O'Connor asked, "How did she react?"

"How did she react?" Cox made a face as if the answer was obvious. "She hired him!"

Now the courtroom really exploded.

John W. Davis stood up, chuckling. "Mr. Cox, besides your obvious sense of humor, what are your academic credentials?"

"Not much," Cox said. "Undergrad degree from College Park and an MBA from UMBC, both earned without distinction."

"As to your MBA, did you attend the graduation ceremony?"

"Of course!"

"With Mr. Jefferson?"

The grin faded from Cox's face. "No. He did not attend."

"Why not?"

"Why are you asking me when you obviously know the answer?"

Davis gestured at the jury. "They need to know too."

Cox looked at Thump, who nodded and smiled. "Unfortunately," Cox said, "my friend did not graduate."

"Why?"

"He couldn't pass the Business Law course, which was a requirement for graduation. Professor Crow failed him three times." Cox turned halfway to face the jury. "There was a rumor that Professor Crow's grandfather was Jim Crow, from the South—"

"Mr. Cox!" Davis pointed a finger at him. "The witness stand is where you testify under oath about facts, not rumors!"

"It's a fact," Cox said, "that there was a rumor at UMBC—"

"That's enough," Judge Clarence said. "Any reference to Jim Crow will be stricken from the record. Proceed, Mr. Davis."

"Thank you," Davis said. "Now, as a self-employed investment advisor, aren't you envious of KKG?"

"Yes."

"And therefore eager to hurt an enviable competitor?"

"Competitor? Me and KKG?" Cox pointed at himself and then at the KKG partners at the defense table. "That's ridiculous. I couldn't possibly compete with KKG."

"You couldn't possibly compete with KKG," Davis repeated. "And is that because of KKG's superior prestige and premiere reputation?"

"No, it's because I don't have the physical attributes to thump rich widows."

Judge Clarence hit his gavel repeatedly to silence the laughter.

At the defense table, Goldberg buried his face in his hands.

CHAPTER 42

Tiffany took the witness stand looking both beautiful and sad. She stated her name, took the oath, and sat upright, her dark eyes bearing into O'Connor, who wasted no time:

"Please describe your relationship with Mr. Jefferson."

"I met his mother first," Tiffany said. "At the hospital. We became friends, and she told me about her son, how wonderful he is and all that. I thought, yeah, right! Another loser with a blind mother—"

The audience laughed.

"But you went out with him?"

"I didn't want to hurt her feelings."

"How did it turn out?"

"We met, and to my great surprise, he was everything she'd said he was."

There was more laughter.

"He was smart and polite. A real gentleman. And funny too!"

"You dated him?"

"Yes. We had a great time together. When he made vice president, he proposed marriage to me."

Tiffany's eyes met Thump's, and she quickly looked away.

O'Connor made a note in her pad. "When did you hear that he was injured?"

"A nurse called me from the ER. I ran down, found doctors working on him."

"What was his condition?"

"He was bloody and unconscious. He had multiple fractures in his leg and hip. They took him into surgery. I waited with Mrs. Jefferson until the surgeons came out. They put him back together, but there was extensive damage, and there's always the risk of a post surgery embolism, even months later."

"Did they tell you about his long-term prognosis?"

Tiffany hesitated. "There's no way to know how long it will take before he can walk again, and how well, even if there are no other complications."

Davis was up and going before O'Connor even sat down. He walked back and forth in front of the jury box as if making sure they realized he was about to expose important facts.

"Before you accepted Mr. Jefferson's engagement proposal," Davis said, "did you set a condition?"

"Yes," Tiffany said.

"What was it?"

"I asked for a vow of fidelity."

"Because you knew he slept around?"

"Women were hot for him, I knew that."

"But it wasn't these women that you asked to take a vow of fidelity," Davis said. "It was your fiancé. Why?"

"To make it clear what his obligation to me was, even when there's overwhelming temptation."

"Overwhelming?" Davis's voice hinted of sarcasm. "Is it really that hard for a man to resist women's advances?"

Tiffany looked him up and down. "You haven't experienced women's advances?"

Laughter exploded in the courtroom, and even the judge smiled.

Davis smiled. "But still, why a vow and not just a promise? Did you not trust him to keep a regular promise?"

"Marriage is a vow," she said, serious again. "So this needed to be a vow also."

"Did you expect him to cheat anyway?"

"Why should I? He's not a lawyer."

"Very funny." Davis rolled his eyes. "Did it bother you that he was known for being uniquely well endowed?"

"Sir, in my line of work I've seen them better endowed than your arm."

The fat black juror laughed loudly, which turned out to be contagious, and soon the whole jury box was laughing.

Davis waited until silence returned. "But in the end, he did cheat on you, didn't he?"

The question was like a spear that went through Tiffany, deflating her. "Yes. He did."

"How did you find out?"

There was a long silence as Tiffany struggled to keep her composure. "I found discarded panties in the hallway bathroom. The monogram initials were *HDK*, so I knew it was hers." Tiffany pointed at Kingman, seated at the defense table.

"That's preposterous," Davis said. "How could you possibly know who was the owner of the discarded panties? The initials could belong to any one of thousands of names—"

"I recognized her perfume."

Shocked for a moment, Davis recovered quickly. "Have you been professionally trained to recognize scents?"

The whole courtroom waited for her answer with bated breath.

Finally Tiffany said, "I'm a woman and a nurse. I know it when I smell it."

CHAPTER 43

O'Connor, Jerald, and Thump went across the street to have lunch at a busy deli. The crowd was mostly lawyers and their clients, as well as court staff on break.

"I was wondering," Thump said, "why you didn't press Kingman for more."

O'Connor continued eating.

"When she said no to having pressured me, why didn't you go after her? Ask her about what happened—"

"A piece of advice," Jerald said with a grin. "My wife doesn't like to be questioned about her professional decisions. I speak from experience."

"I don't mean it as criticism," Thump said. "I know you haven't practiced law in a long time, and it takes a lot to be able to examine a witness, think on your feet while everyone's watching. I thought you let Kingman get off easy—"

"I have my reasons," O'Connor said. "Do you want to represent yourself?"

"No."

"Then let me do my job."

They ate in awkward silence for a while.

"Did you see," O'Connor said, "how Davis jumped and objected as soon as I asked Kingman about her hoarseness? What's with that?"

"It's a chronic condition," Thump said. "Has to do with her vocal cords. I asked her once about it and she wouldn't say, only smiled in this cryptic way, like there was a story behind it that she can't tell."

"We could," Jerald spoke with his mouth full, "ask for her medical records."

"Waste of time," O'Connor said. "Davis will object, say it's irrelevant. Which it probably is."

"There's one possibility," Thump said. "I can search the fire department's online records of incident reports for her home address and the KKG building. If this hoarseness was ever a cause for calling nine-one-one, I might be able to get details about it."

They looked at him, surprised.

"It's useful data for an investment advisor. For example, a heart attack in a well-to-do neighborhood could mean that a fresh widow now needs help with managing financial assets that her recently departed husband used to handle."

O'Connor shook her head, but Jerald laughed. "Humanitarian aid," he said. "How charitable!"

"Forget it," O'Connor said. "What are we talking about here? Hoarseness isn't a crime."

"Maybe, but we have to find something," Thump said. "Anything that will get to her, get under her skin, peel off her façade, show the jury that she's not this perfect petite lady whose only vices are hard work and perseverance."

"This case is not a personal vendetta," O'Connor said. "Our goal is not to hurt Henrietta Kingman. Our goal is to win a monetary judgment against KKG, that's it."

"I agree," Thump said. "But to win, you'll have to break Kingman."

"Breaking her could backfire."

"How?"

"Sex cases," O'Connor said, "are founded on bias. The woman is always presumed to be the victim. Historically, that's actually been the case. Men were the bosses, women were at their mercy. We're talking centuries of male dominance and female abuse. That's the basis for the assumption, or the cliché, if you like, of us being the weaker gender, of our feminine mystique, all those patronizing terms. And that's why, in this case, the jury's basic instinct is to excuse Kingman's actions and blame you—a big, strong, handsome man, full of confidence, aggression, and virility. Breaking her, therefore, would do us no good. It could actually reaffirm her victim status."

"We might as well drop the case," Thump said. "We can't win if I'm the only bad guy left standing."

"That's correct." O'Connor took a bite from her sandwich and chewed.

Thump and Jerald looked at her.

"Kolbe," O'Connor finally said. "He is the figurehead, the image of KKG—dependable, capable, honorable. That's his shtick, but I have a feeling there's more. He is the one I must break."

"Mr. Kolbe?" Thump laughed. "You want to break Daniel S. Kolbe?"

O'Connor nodded and took another big bite out of her sandwich.

"Huh!" Thump gestured in dismissal. "You'll never manage to break him."

CHAPTER 44

Sharon Boulder wore a cream dress, earth-toned makeup, and no jewelry except for a simple pearl necklace. Her hair was pulled back into a ponytail. She projected the model image of a widow who was aging yet dignified, timid yet poised, and affluent yet modest.

"Mrs. Boulder," O'Connor said, "as chairperson of the Boulder Trust, were you happy with the work performed by Thump?"

"Do you mean Mr. Jefferson?"

"Correct."

"I can't really say. In my volunteer work for my late husband's charitable trust, I usually communicate with the senior partners at KKG."

"That would make sense, yes, it would." O'Connor glanced at a document. "But I'm a bit confused here, looking at an e-mail from you to Henrietta Kingman, sent after a court hearing, that said: '*Thump's quick input was key to victory. He's the alpha male.*' Did you mean Mr. Jefferson?"

"Oh goodness." Boulder smiled demurely. "Did someone hack into my personal e-mails?"

"We obtained it as part of the discovery," O'Connor said. "Now, about this e-mail—"

"Henrietta and I are old friends. We silly girls joke around about things. For fun. It's silly, but you know how it is."

"Speaking of fun, did you ever pressure Mr. Jefferson for sex?"

Davis got up. "Objection! Speculative!"

Judge Clarence looked at O'Connor. "Counselor?"

"Your Honor?" O'Connor looked back at him in defiance.

There was a long silence during which they held eye contact, until the judge chuckled, breaking the tension. "Perhaps," he said, "we should switch places, and you can come up here and hold the gavel."

Everyone laughed.

"If my esteemed colleague," O'Connor said, pointing in Davis's direction, "is going to jump up and cry foul every time I utter the word 'sex' as part of a question, then, with all due sympathy to his puritanical sensibilities, this case might be the wrong subject matter for him to litigate."

"Fair enough," Judge Clarence said. "I'll allow the question. But you're on a short leash. Notwithstanding your client's serious allegations in the complaint, this judicial process is about proving your case with admissible evidence, not insinuations and raunchy innuendo."

"Thank you!" Davis sat down.

"In other words," Judge Clarence said, "I won't permit you to abuse witnesses on the flimsy premise that you could dredge up circumstantial evidence otherwise absent from the record."

"Fair enough," O'Connor said. "Mrs. Boulder, the question was simple. Did you ever pressure Mr. Jefferson for sex?"

"No."

"Let me juggle your memory. When he came to your house to show the presentation, did he tell you that he had gotten engaged?"

"I don't recall."

Picking another document from the table, O'Connor said, "Here's a different e-mail from you to Henrietta Kingman—"

"Wait, I don't understand." Sharon Boulder looked at Davis. "These are personal e-mails."

"Let me clarify." O'Connor examined her notes. "As part of our discovery in this case, we requested and received copies of all correspondence between KKG and the Boulder Trust. Your e-mails to Miss Kingman came from the account of the trust: Chair@BoulderTrust.org. As such, these e-mails were subject to production as part of the discovery."

The judge looked at Davis, who said nothing.

"Now," O'Connor continued, "one day before the board meeting, you sent this e-mail to Miss Kingman: '*Thump came with the presentation, a fine spiel. Per your advice, I insisted on a climax. He entered via the back door. OMG! He's so big, the door frame almost burst!*' Did you send this e-mail?"

The full courtroom watched Sharon Boulder in silence as she struggled to answer.

"Yes," she finally said. "I sent this e-mail."

"Thank you." O'Connor looked at the paper closely. "When you wrote '*I insisted on a climax,*' what did you mean?"

"The presentation needed a stronger conclusion, that's what I meant by climax." Boulder spoke fast, redness rising from her neck.

"And when you wrote '*He entered via the back door,*' what did you mean?"

"It's the service entrance, in the back of the house. We use our front door only for social functions."

"Is that so?" O'Connor put down the document and picked up a memory flash drive that had an oversized red tag dangling from it on a ring. "Are you aware of the scope and capture area of your next door neighbor's security cameras?"

Boulder looked at Davis, who said nothing. She had no choice but to answer.

"No."

"Let's see." O'Connor turned to the court deputy. "Can we get a TV in here?"

"Excuse me!" Boulder turned to the judge. "I'm not feeling well!"

"Your Honor," Davis said, "I'd like to request a short recess to view these videos. We were not given copies during discovery."

"I don't object," O'Connor said. "As long as I can ask the witness a couple of brief questions before we take a break."

Judge Clarence nodded. "Make it quick."

"Mrs. Boulder," O'Connor said, rattling the tagged memory flash drive, "bearing in mind the criminal ramifications of lying on the witness stand, please think carefully before you answer. When Mr. Jefferson came to your house to show you the PowerPoint presentation, did he enter through the front door?"

After a long pause, Boulder answered quietly, "Yes."

O'Connor stepped closer to the witness stand. "In the e-mail to Henrietta Kingman, when you wrote that '*He entered via the back door,*' were you referring to your anus?"

Looking down, Boulder mumbled something.

Judge Clarence said, "The witness will answer yes or no."

Barely audible, she said, "Yes."

The audience groaned, and the jury members looked at each other, then at Thump, who kept his eyes fixed on the table before him, not moving except for his chest, which rose and sank with his accelerating breaths.

After a moment Tiffany couldn't hold it anymore and started crying. She got up, made her way down the row of spectators, and ran down the aisle and out of the courtroom.

Mrs. Jefferson, wiping her eyes, followed her.

CHAPTER 45

Dressed in shorts and a T-shirt, Thump rolled his wheelchair to the dining table, which his mother had already set for their dinner with two bowls of salad and a pitcher of iced tea.

Mrs. Jefferson glanced at him. "Have you done your exercises yet?"

"No." He unfolded his napkin.

"You must do the daily exercises or—"

"I don't have the energy for it, OK?"

His sharp tone didn't faze her. "Remember what Dr. Cohen said about being lazy and not moving around after a major surgery?"

Thump picked at his salad.

"Especially with multiple bone fractures." Mrs. Jefferson poured dressing over her salad. "He said that being sedentary is like playing Russian roulette. And with high stress on top of it, he said you could suffer—"

"He's a surgeon. He parrots the same warnings to every patient."

"And they listen to him!"

"I listened. He sounded like an actor in one of those commercials for Lipitor or Viagra, reciting the laundry list of risk factors."

"He was doing no commercial for Viagra. He was talking to you about surviving. Risk factors are for real. I see patients in the hospital every day—"

"Poor Dr. Cohen." Pushing his salad bowl away, Thump sneered. "He's probably afraid I'll sue him too."

Mrs. Jefferson pushed his salad bowl back toward him. "If I can stand in the kitchen and cut vegetables after sitting in that fancy courtroom all day and hearing such awful things about you, then you can eat what I made!"

He obliged her, forking a piece of lettuce and putting it in his mouth.

"And you're going to do the exercises every day, like Dr. Cohen said, because I don't want to be stuck here taking care of you for the rest of my life!"

He picked a piece of tomato. "I thought you liked vegetables."

"Don't you get smart with me, Thurgood Marshall Jefferson! If you cause your own demise then—so help me God!—I will ship you off to an institute where you can drool all day and pee in a plastic bag! You got that?"

"Yes, Mother." Thump held his salad bowl with exaggerated eagerness and speared a bunch on his fork, stuffing his mouth.

She shook her head, huffing disapprovingly.

When they finished eating, as she was clearing the plates, Thump asked, "Will Tiffany come back to court tomorrow?"

"Do you want her there?"

"I need her there. If she hears the witnesses, what was going on, she might understand that it wasn't so simple for me to say no."

Mrs. Jefferson grunted.

"Did she tell you if she's coming back?" He rolled after his mother into the kitchen. "Did you talk to her?"

"I gave her a shoulder to cry on." Mrs. Jefferson started doing the dishes. "Talking is your business."

"She won't speak with me."

"But she'll listen."

"You think?"

"What I think is that she's working tonight. That's what I think."

CHAPTER 46

On the eighth floor at Baltimore Memorial Hospital, Thump maneuvered the wheelchair to the tall counter at the nurses' station. He grabbed the edge and lifted himself, his weight resting on his left leg.

Tiffany, seated behind the counter, looked up, and her eyes widened.

Thump smiled. "Hi."

She got up and turned to leave.

"Wait!"

She paused.

"Hear me out. One minute, that's all. Please?"

Still not looking at him, Tiffany stayed put.

"I don't blame you for being angry with me." Thump started to slide sideways, but he managed to shift his position and lean against the counter. "The more I allow myself to think about what I had to do during the last five years, the more I hate myself."

She made a sound of agreement.

"This whole trial, it's horrible. I want to drop it, run away. No sum of money's worth it. And it's not the money I'm doing it for. It's not!"

Finally she looked at him.

"The only thing," Thump said, his voice breaking, "the only thing that keeps me going is the chance to make you understand why I did it, what it was really like."

CHAPTER 47

KKG's Human Resources Director Tecumseh Tekatawa took the witness stand with her long hair loose, her Native American necklaces prominent, and her nervousness visible.

O'Connor approached her. "Could you please describe your work at KKG?"

"I've been HR director for three years. We have about fifty investment professionals and a hundred support staff. I'm responsible for all aspects of employment, such as payroll, benefits, compliance with laws and regulations, resolution of any complaints or issues with employees, things like that."

"Were there any employment issues with Mr. Jefferson?"

"Not until he was dismissed. He had worked hard, always friendly, funny—"

Thump glanced over his shoulder, his eyes searching the audience until he found Tiffany, seated next to his mother.

"As far as you knew," O'Connor said, "was he sexually active within KKG?"

"There were jokes," Tecumseh said, "rumors, but nothing specific. No complaints about him."

"What happened after the last meeting in Mr. Kolbe's office, when he was fired?"

"I brought a cardboard box with his personal belongings from his office and gave him his last paycheck. I took his card key and accompanied him out."

"That's it? On the spot?"

"Yes."

"No chance to say good-bye to his assistant? His colleagues?"

Tecumseh shook her head. "It's firm policy. A terminated employee must leave the building immediately."

"Isn't it harsh?"

"It's standard in the financial industry. Our first duty is to protect clients' financial confidentiality."

"No good-byes, then." O'Connor waited a moment to let this piece of information sink in. "What happened then?"

"We went down the elevator to the ground floor."

"I see. Now, backing up for a moment. How did you know to prepare for it?"

"Mr. Kolbe had told me that Mr. Jefferson would be dismissed. While they met with him, I was to have his computer access terminated, box up his personal effects, and prepare his final paycheck."

"So the meeting was merely a formality, not an opportunity for him to explain or save his job somehow?"

"That was my understanding."

"Didn't you question Mr. Kolbe about it?"

"He didn't ask for my opinion. It wasn't my place to defend Thump."

"After five years of working together? It seems a bit heartless, doesn't it?"

Tecumseh shrugged. "Part of the job."

"Here's your stuff, here's your last paycheck, and here's the door?"

"Honestly, it's easier to cut things off quickly. No long farewells, no unpleasantness."

The jurors looked at each other, visibly disapproving.

"By the way," O'Connor said, "have you experienced prejudice at KKG?"

"Not directly."

"Indirectly then?"

"Like in many established companies, our firm's culture is slow to change."

"Could you be more specific?"

"KKG has always catered to a certain type of clientele—very rich, very traditional, and very white. These people expect their financial advisors to mirror their social and cultural world."

"What about rich black clients?"

"Athletes and rappers?" Tecumseh smiled. "I'm sure their assets are managed by firms whose culture fits their personal comfort zone."

The exchange put the whole courtroom in a tense silence, and the three black jurors looked at each other.

"I'd like to clarify," Tecumseh said, "that we are working to change the firm's culture. The business environment is changing, and we must change."

"How so?"

"My role as HR director is to direct the hiring process. These days, KKG's strategy is aimed at earning large contracts to manage institutional money, such as pension funds, which often have minorities in high management positions. To succeed in that environment, we have to diversify our pool of investment advisors and, eventually, partner ranks."

"Going back to my original question," O'Connor said, "have you experienced any personal prejudice at KKG?"

"I heard that Mr. Kolbe commented on my hairstyle, that it's too ethnic and not very professional."

Everyone laughed, including Mr. Kolbe.

Davis started his cross-examination with a no-nonsense, simple question: "During your time at KKG, how many complaints of racial or sexual discrimination have you received?"

"None," Tecumseh said.

"How often did you see Mr. Jefferson?"

"Every day. Our offices were nearby."

"Did you speak often?"

"Yes. All the time."

"All the time," Davis repeated. "About what?"

"Everything—work, business, movies, sports."

"And during these years of daily, frequent contact, during all these wonderful conversations, has this plaintiff," Davis pointed at Thump, "ever complained to you about any of the scandalous facts he now claims in this licentious case?"

"Not explicitly."

"Let me clarify the question," Davis said. "Has Plaintiff ever complained, explicitly or implicitly, verbally or literally? Had he ever mentioned that a partner pressured him for sex? Yes or no?"

"No."

"Thank you!" Davis turned to the jury, raised his arms dramatically, and returned to his seat.

O'Connor browsed through her notes, giving the impression that she wasn't sure there was anything more she wanted to ask Tecumseh.

"This should be an easy question to answer," she said, rising slowly. "Were you sexually attracted to Thump?"

Tecumseh opened her mouth to answer, but Davis was quicker. "Objection! Irrelevant!"

"I'll withdraw the question," O'Connor said. "It seems that my opponent has a real aversion to any questions that include the word sex. Let me instead ask you a less explicit question, which you can answer factually with a yes or a no. During the time of your acquaintance with Thump, have you ever craved his crowned cock?"

The audience groaned collectively, and Davis yelled, "Objection!"

"Sustained," the judge said.

"Withdrawn," O'Connor said. "Have you ever glimpsed his giant genitals?"

"Objection!"

"Sustained!"

"Have you ever gagged on his glorious geyser?"

"Objection!"

"Sustained!"

"Or did you," O'Connor raised her voice, "just go for a good gut-wrenching thump in your back door?"

Davis was shouting now, "Objection! Objection! Objection!"

"Sustained!" Judge Clarence glared at O'Connor. "What the hell was that? You better explain!"

Stepping forward, closer to the judge, O'Connor still spoke loudly enough for everyone to hear her. "This case is about sex. That's what everyone is thinking about." She gestured at the crowded courtroom. "They want to know about my client, about his thumping, about KKG's partners and staff and clients. Every person in this courtroom is wondering: Who got it? How did they get it? Where did they get it? And what nasty things did they do in order to get it, or to give it?"

Davis showed his hands in a silent plea to the judge.

"And it's not only about my client," O'Connor said. "Or about sex per se. It's about much more than that. What happened to him at KKG is a direct consequence of our loathing and fear and envy of black men. It's about the love-hate relationship that festers at KKG and simmers in many other companies and organizations. It's about our giddy obsession with the myth of black men's sexual prowess and our anxious presumption that they're predisposed to violence. That's what this case is about, so let's stop beating around the bush, no pun intended—"

"Enough!" Judge Clarence pulled off his eyeglasses and used them to jab at O'Connor. "Counselor! In this courtroom, which happens to be presided over by a black man, we are color blind!"

"Your Honor," O'Connor said, "even those who are color blind can tell black from white."

CHAPTER 48

O'Connor and Jerald went back to the office that evening to prepare for the next day of trial. They stopped by the Bar Bar Pub to get a quick dinner. The place was packed with lawyers and other professionals who by now were nursing their second or third drink. Sitting at the bar, O'Connor and Jerald ordered cheeseburgers and fries. On the TV above their heads, which was tuned to the evening news, footage appeared of Davis leaving the courthouse with the KKG partners, raising his hand to block off the reporters.

A middle-aged white lawyer, taking a swig from a Samuel Adams bottle, said to O'Connor, "Your opponent isn't happy today."

She nodded, biting into her cheeseburger.

"Looks like you've learned some nasty tricks from us trial lawyers appearing before you all those years."

O'Connor swallowed and said, "You betcha."

A black lawyer across the bar put down his drink. "Aren't you bothered by your client's 'culture of victimhood and entitlement'—to borrow your own infamous words?"

"No, his entitlement doesn't bother me, because when he wins the case, I'll be entitled to a contingency fee of forty percent."

Everyone laughed, and the barman raised a full glass at her before handing it to one of the customers.

"Forty percent, huh?" The black lawyer sneered. "So it's all about money to you?"

Jerald put a hand on her forearm, but O'Connor replied anyway. "Sir, don't take my jest out of context. Money's important.

We've got to eat. But for me it's always about the law. My client was abused—"

"Allegedly. You want to know what I think? I think it was plain old office sex, romping fun, totally innocuous, which he's now blowing out of proportion for the purpose of financial gain."

"Office sex between a partner and a junior employee is not done for fun."

"Sex is sex. It's either fun or rape, and he wasn't raped by a woman half his size."

"Then you'd have no problem asking your secretary to kneel down and blow you?"

"My secretary is my wife. She blows me off every time I ask for anything."

Roaring with laughter, the lawyers around the bar toasted him.

"Your client," the white lawyer at her side said, "isn't some cute secretary. He's a big, strong fellow—"

"So what? If your secretary is a big, strong woman, is she fair game? Are strong people not afraid of losing their jobs? Of being cheated out of a promotion?"

No one responded to that.

"My client," O'Connor continued, "got himself through school and built a career by working his ass off—"

"Wasn't his ass he worked off." The white lawyer signaled the bartender for another bottle of Samuel Adams.

"Ha." The black lawyer hit the bar. "You white boys are jealous." He made a fist, raising it. "Black power!"

"Shhh!" Jerald pointed to the TV.

The TV reporter was saying, "—in an e-mail to the media, an official at Teachers' Pension Fund stated that KKG will be dropped from consideration for an investment management contract if the firm is held liable for sexual harassment."

CHAPTER 49

O'Connor reviewed her notes, then approached the witness stand, which was occupied by Thump's former assistant, Andy.

"Did you help Mr. Jefferson prepare the PowerPoint presentation?"

"Yes," Andy said.

"Did you write it?"

"No. Mr. Jefferson wrote the text. All the slides, he created them. I did the research, based on the parameters that he gave me in terms of the companies' types of industries and markets and the ways they do business, how they matched the social goals of the Boulder Trust, and we also looked for financial strength and potential for growth."

"Very good," O'Connor said. "Now, did you see the presentation after it was complete?"

Andy thought for a moment. "Only parts of it, looking over Mr. Jefferson's shoulder, that kind of thing."

"And on that last Friday morning, after you called him to say it was missing from his laptop, what happened?"

"He raced to the office. We searched every file on his laptop. He was so upset. It was terrible!" Suddenly Andy was struggling not to cry. "I'm sorry," he said, choking. "It was a very difficult day, the worst—"

"Take your time." O'Connor handed him a glass of water.

Andy took a sip, inhaled deeply, and put down the glass.

"In your opinion," O'Connor said, "was he a good investment manager?"

"I don't know. He was a good boss."

The audience chuckled.

"Did partners criticize his work?"

"I wouldn't hear even if they did."

"Why?"

"KKG culture is very proper, very polite." Andy smiled. "At least on the surface."

"Did Mr. Jefferson have sex with clients?"

Davis rose to object, but O'Connor quickly clarified:

"In your personal knowledge?"

Andy hesitated, clearly embarrassed. "I took calls for him."

"Did they mention sex?"

"Some voice messages were explicit."

"For example?"

"There was one woman, a couple of weeks before Mr. Jefferson left." Andy looked around, then back at O'Connor. "She was so funny, I actually memorized it."

"Go ahead."

In a feminine, seductive tone, Andy quoted the message: "Thanks for a most stimulating meeting yesterday. Loved your approach to investments and your focus on hard numbers. You're a straight shooter, and I can't wait to explore various holding positions with you, have you manage my liquid assets, maybe thump in a big deposit? Call me!"

The Asian woman juror giggled into her hands while the others laughed openly.

Andy's face was red. "I don't remember her name, but it was so—"

"Memorable," O'Connor said. "Indeed. Now, since you're already blushing, let me ask you a personal question. Has Mr. Jefferson ever thumped you?"

Davis said, "Objection!"

"I wouldn't mind," Andy said.

Everyone laughed, and Thump shook a finger at him.

Judge Clarence waited for silence and said to Andy, "If you hear an objection, don't answer until I rule on it."

"Sorry," Andy said.

O'Connor sat down, and Davis rose to conduct his cross-examination.

"Andy," Davis said, "when did you become an assistant to the plaintiff?"

"When Mr. Jefferson was promoted to associate. I think it was about three years before he was fired from the firm."

"How often did he go out during work days to meet with women?"

The question threw Andy off balance, and he looked at the judge before answering. "I don't know. I didn't take count."

"Give me a ballpark number," Davis said. "Was it once a year? Once a month? Once a week?"

"Yeah, probably once a week, or two weeks."

"Thank you." Davis smiled. "That would be between twenty-five and fifty times per year, right?"

"Do you want me to do the math now?"

The audience laughed.

"You do know there are about fifty weeks in a year, yes?"

"Yes."

"And fifty times three is one hundred and fifty, correct?"

"Yes."

"That means that you saw Mr. Jefferson leave the office to cavort with women during working hours a total of between seventy-five and one hundred and fifty times over your three years together, correct?"

"I guess so," Andy said.

"That's a lot of cavorting." Davis paced back and forth before asking his next question. "Now, over those three years of working together, and with all those trysts during working hours, and with all those salacious voice messages, has Mr. Jefferson ever complained of being pressured to sleep with women?"

"Not explicitly."

"Here we go again." Davis exhaled loudly. "Please answer the question. Did he ever complain?"

"Mr. Jefferson would never complain. It wasn't his style."

"His style? What's that supposed to mean?"

"He's not a complainer," Andy said. "That's the most important thing I learned from him—"

"Thank you." Davis raised his hand. "I didn't ask what you learned from the plaintiff."

As Davis sat, O'Connor got up for redirect.

"Andy," O'Connor said with a hint of a smile. "What was the most important thing that you learned from Mr. Jefferson during your three years of working together?"

Davis started to rise, but Judge Clarence looked at him with an expression that made him change his mind and remain seated.

"Never to complain," Andy said. "He worked hard and took the good with the bad, did whatever he had to do, eyes on the target. And he kept trying different strategies to find his own clients in order to be more independent. If one thing didn't work out, he'd try another. And when someone made a snide remark, he would just laugh it off." Andy was on the verge of crying again.

"Take your time," O'Connor said.

Andy took a sip of water. "He's my role model. I want to be like him."

"In what way?"

"To be strong, to know my own worth even if others bear prejudice against me or against the person they think I am."

"Thank you for sharing this," O'Connor said.

Andy nodded.

"Now I want to go back to the math exercise about all these women that he was meeting. Who were they?"

"Potential clients, or existing clients too. Most of them were connected to Henrietta Kingman in one way or another."

"What was the nature of the relationship between Miss Kingman and Mr. Jefferson?"

"Their relationship?" Andy considered the question. "She was the boss, I mean, she's second only to Mr. Kolbe himself, who is like God at KKG."

"Did Mr. Jefferson work with her more than with other partners?"

"Yes. It wasn't a formal thing, but everybody knew that Mr. Jefferson was her favorite. They did a lot of marketing together."

"Such as?"

"Miss Kingman often took him along to meet with potential clients. Usually they were women whom she identified as good prospects for investment management services. Sometimes she'd send him alone. And we often received phone calls from women who had gotten his number from Miss Kingman."

"How did he deal with it?"

"The same way he dealt with everything else," Andy said.

"Which is?"

"Enthusiastically."

The audience laughed.

"I wasn't asking about his personal style," O'Connor said. "What I would like to know is whether or not Mr. Jefferson ever tried to avoid Miss Kingman?"

"Only in the last week."

"Do you speak from personal knowledge?"

"He asked me to make sure he's not stuck with her alone."

"Stuck?"

"That's the word he used."

Andy glanced at Henrietta Kingman, who was shaking her head, her face showing disgust.

"Did you succeed?"

"She came over to Mr. Jefferson's office a few times. We had to move to an open conference room where she couldn't corner him."

"Does Miss Kingman have a nickname at KKG?"

Andy glanced at the KKG partners before answering. "Hot Damn."

Kingman, at the defense table, laughed with everyone else.

"And you," O'Connor said, "do you have a nickname at KKG?"

"Some people call me Andus."

O'Connor struggled not to laugh. "How about Miss Tekatawa?"

"Tecumseh? We call her Twin Peaks."

"For her birthplace?"

"Not really."

Tecumseh, in a back row, rolled her eyes.

"How about Mr. Kolbe?"

Andy was reluctant. "Sometime we call him Mr. Kock."

"That's straightforward. And Mr. Goldberg?"

"He's called Fussin."

"For being fussy?"

"No," Andy said. "It's the circumcision."

"Oh, I see. Fussin for foreskin. They almost rhyme. And Mr. Chang?"

"He's known as Wii."

"For the video game?"

"Not really. It's Wii as an acronym: Where is it?"

The redneck juror laughed harder than anyone else, except maybe the Asian woman juror, who covered her face with her purse in a failed attempt to hide behind it.

After dinner, Thump used his mother's aging desktop computer to pull up the Internet site for the *City of Baltimore, Fire Department.* In the search box for *Accident Reports,* he typed in the address for the KKG building: *6584 S. Charles Street.* He squinted at the screen, which showed the data in very small print, then clicked on *Print,* and the old printer began to rattle.

CHAPTER 50

First thing in the morning, O'Connor called Bo Chang as a witness. He took the oath and sat down, nodding at the judge with a smile, completely at ease.

"Please," O'Connor said, "tell us about your professional history."

"It's a short history. I came from Korea, earned a PhD in finance, joined KKG as an analyst, received annual promotions, and eventually became a partner four years ago."

"Do you have a specialty?"

"Foreign currency trades, interest-bearing products, and tax-driven securities."

"Who was handling these areas before you came along?"

"No one. But KKG was starting to grow and needed wider areas of expertise among its investment advisory team."

"Miss Tekatawa mentioned a strategy to expand into handling large, institutional money."

"That's correct."

"Why?"

Chang laughed, as if the answer was obvious. "More assets under management, more fees."

O'Connor looked at her notes. "Besides your responsibilities to clients, aren't you also chair of the diversity committee at KKG?"

"That's correct."

"Why does KKG need a diversity committee?"

"We are an equal opportunity employer. There's issues of compliance with federal regulations, state law requirements—"

Chang paused, seeing Davis whisper in Mr. Kolbe's ear.

"Besides legal compliance," O'Connor said, "are there other reasons that KKG needs a diversity committee with a partner running it?"

"Business reasons," Chang said. "The most important one is that large pension funds expect to see a real commitment to diversity from firms that are considered for investment management contracts. By having a full-blown diversity committee, we show that we're putting a lot of effort into it."

"And how is the firm's diversity effort going? Not only secretaries and janitors, but among the professionals, the investment advisors?"

Davis got up. "Objection. Vague and unclear."

"Sustained," the judge said.

"I'll rephrase." O'Connor looked at her notes. "Other than Mr. Jefferson, have there been any African American investment professionals working at KKG?"

Davis was still on his feet. "Objection. Irrelevant. This is not a race discrimination case. KKG's hiring statistics are irrelevant."

Judge Clarence looked at O'Connor.

"Relevancy," she argued, "is to be judged expansively. Plaintiff's work conditions are relevant, and KKG's history with respect to African American employees is relevant, especially as we live in a city where African Americans have made great strides, rising to senior positions in politics and," she gestured at the judge, "the judicial system."

"Thank you for pointing that out to me." Judge Clarence smirked. "Mr. Davis, would you like to respond to this argument?"

"My concern," Davis said, "is that Plaintiff's counsel keeps trying to play the race card here, which I find distasteful, opportunistic, and demeaning not only to her own client, but to everyone else here." He paused and glanced meaningfully at his African American associate, Erica Dropper. "We don't live in the nineteen sixties anymore. The court should not allow my opponent to artificially inseminate this case with seeds of interracial tensions. This trial is about the plaintiff's sexual promiscuity. That's it."

"Your Honor," O'Connor said. "To argue that my client's harassment and termination was not impacted by racism is like arguing that the Reverend Dr. Martin Luther King Jr. was killed by a stray bullet."

Judge Clarence sighed. "I'll allow the question. Please repeat it to remind the witness."

"The question was this," O'Connor said. "Other than the plaintiff, have there been any other African American investment professionals working at KKG?"

Chang hesitated. "We have not been able to hire a qualified African American candidate yet, despite the fact that we've extended several offers."

"In your experience as chair of the diversity committee, what is the reason for this?"

"We have a certain reputation in the community."

"Such as?"

"Our business model until recently was to provide investment management services to high-net-worth individuals and families. It's not like government or politics. It's not a democracy. These clients have many choices, other investment management firms. Wealthy clients are highly selective, even finicky—"

"You mean, they're white."

Chang shifted uncomfortably. "Yes, for the most part. But the world is changing, and we're determined to change with it."

"In what way?"

"We're aiming to win large institutional clients, such as pension funds, to reduce our dependency on wealthy individuals and families. For that purpose, my committee is working to change KKG's image with respect to diversity—"

"And what about sexual harassment?"

"That doesn't require a committee."

Everyone laughed.

"Another thing," O'Connor said, "that doesn't require a committee is sabotaging a colleague's computer, you agree?"

"Are you asking me," Chang said, "or is this a rhetorical question?"

"Let me clarify. According to security cameras, on that particular Friday morning, the only people who came in before Andy were you and Henrietta Kingman."

"I always come in early."

"I haven't asked a question yet."

O'Connor took her time. Chang shifted in the seat, but continued to project an almost giddy air of careless irreverence.

"My question is," O'Connor finally said, "did you touch Mr. Jefferson's laptop that morning?"

"No."

"Did you see anyone else touch it?"

"No, and I don't think anyone touched it."

"Why do you think so?"

"Because he showed us a draft of the presentation that missed a lot of numbers—and to me, numbers are everything. Then he had a big party at his place that night and no time to finish the job, so he deleted it and started whining." Chang looked down at Thump. "That's what I think."

With sudden rage, Thump pushed back his wheelchair, banging it against a railing.

O'Connor signaled to him to calm down and asked Chang, "Do you dislike Mr. Jefferson?"

"No."

"Weren't you jealous of him?"

"Jealous? Why should I be?" Chang laughed. "I'm a lot smarter."

"Are you?"

"He couldn't even finish his MBA. I earned a PhD with honors."

"Did it bother you that his nickname was *Thump* and yours was—and I assume still is—*Where is it?*"

Chang's smile faded and he glared at O'Connor. "Did it bother you that lawyers nicknamed you Judge Rob?"

"Please," Judge Clarence said, "answer the question, Mr. Chang."

Chang turned sharply toward the judge. "It's *Doctor* Chang, Judge!"

"Actually," Judge Clarence said, "if we want to insist on formalities, it's *Doctor Judge,* Doctor Chang. Though my PhD is in forensic science, not finance."

Chang turned red. "I apologize."

"Please answer the question, Dr. Chang."

"To remind you," O'Connor said, "the question was whether the fact that your nickname is Wii and his—"

"I remember the question!" Chang was panting now, his voice rising. "And my answer is that I don't care about silly nicknames that come from ignorant people and their prejudice, because I hate all racists!" His eyes burned holes in O'Connor. "I do! I hate racists who say stupid things about other people and, you know, about their cultures!"

In the ensuing silence, the jurors looked at O'Connor, waiting for her to respond.

She hesitated, then turned and went back to her seat. Thump looked at her, but she kept her eyes on her notes.

Davis stood for the cross-examination. "Dr. Chang, how long had you worked with the plaintiff?"

Chang sipped water before answering. "Since he joined KKG."

"What was your relationship with him?"

"The relationship of a partner to a junior employee. We said hello in the hallways when we ran into each other, sometimes went out to lunch with a few other people. We were friendly."

"And during those five years of friendly collegiality, did he ever mention to you or to anyone else in your presence that he was being pressured to engage in sex?"

"Not even once."

Davis turned to the jury, paused to look at them, and returned to his seat.

CHAPTER 51

At the lunch deli near the courthouse, O'Connor and Jerald had ham sandwiches while Thump had a bowl of soup. He took out a piece of paper and unfolded it on the table.

"This is a report from the Baltimore Fire Department."

O'Connor and Jerald continued to eat while looking at it.

"Right here." Thump pointed. "The incidents are listed chronologically, in reverse order, the latest one first."

"Look at this," Jerald said. "*Pedestrian hit by moving vehicle in front of building. Unresponsive, bleeding. Victim is a black male, about thirty.*"

"That was me," Thump said. "And here it says *H&R, R/T BPD.* It's an acronym for *Hit and Run, Reported to Baltimore Police Department.*"

"Scary," Jerald said. "I wonder if the driver even knew he hit you."

"I doubt it," Thump said. "Now the entries below are fire alarm triggers, one, two, three, and so on, total of thirteen. About twice a year. False alarms."

"What's this at the bottom?"

"*Medical Emergency – Caller reported a woman is choking inside the building.*" Thump pointed to the entry. "NFP. That's *No Foul Play.* No police action is mentioned, which means it was some kind of an accident."

Jerald peered at the paper. "But there's no name. Who was choking?"

"Names are redacted for medical confidentiality reasons. All it says is *Victim is white female, late forties.*"

"It's useless information." O'Connor took another bite.

"But look here." Thump placed his finger under the tiny numbers. "See the date?"

Jerald read it along. "*Seven, three—*"

"Yes," Thump said. "July third. How many years ago?"

Looking carefully, Jerald calculated in his head. "Seven. It happened seven years ago!"

O'Connor stopped chewing and looked at the paper with sudden interest.

CHAPTER 52

"Mr. Goldberg." O'Connor approached the witness stand, playing with an oversized pen. "Have you ever observed anything unusual between Henrietta Kingman and Mr. Jefferson?"

Arthur Goldberg adjusted his eyeglasses and looked at John Davis, who looked away, making no objection.

"Unusual?" Goldberg shrugged. "In what way?"

"Compared with your relationship with him."

"I'm not a woman."

The audience laughed.

"You're not a woman," O'Connor said. "I'm relieved to hear that. But why is this fact responsive to my question?"

"Women melted around Thump."

"Are you saying that Miss Kingman melted around Thump?"

"No." Goldberg seemed to shrink behind the witness stand. "I was speaking generally."

"No melting for Kingman?"

"No."

"Then what happened to her around Mr. Jefferson other than melting? Thawing?"

"No."

"Liquefying?"

"No."

"Dissolving?"

"No."

Davis stood. "Your Honor, I was trying to minimize my objections, but this really goes beyond reason. My opponent is practically harassing the witness."

"I'm merely trying," O'Connor said, "to make him answer my questions with clarity, rather than with evasive generalities."

"OK," Judge Clarence said. "Ask your next question."

"My original question, which remains unanswered, was simple: Have you ever observed anything unusual between Henrietta Kingman and Mr. Jefferson?"

"Only thing I can think of," Goldberg said, "is that she occasionally had him stay in her office after meetings."

"And that was unusual?"

"A bit."

"Why? Don't you meet with junior staffers in your office, or ask a young associate to stay after a meeting for additional discussions or assignments?"

Cornered once more, Goldberg blurted, "Not with the door closed."

"You never close your office door?"

"Not when I'm meeting with an attractive young staffer."

"Why?"

"People assume the obvious."

The audience groaned at hearing this. The jurors, all of them simultaneously, turned their heads to look in the direction of the defense table, where Kingman's face remained expressionless.

"Thank you," O'Connor said. "Now, changing subject, I want to know about the view from your office. Can you see the street below?"

"Yes. My office window faces Charles Street."

"Can you see the sidewalk below, at the entrance to the KKG building?"

"Yes."

"Do you recall seeing Mr. Jefferson come and go during working days?"

"Occasionally," Goldberg said.

"Was there any pattern to his coming and going?"

"I guess there was." He hesitated. "I often saw him from my window, down below in the street, get into cars, usually luxury cars. He'd return an hour or two later."

"Different cars?"

"Yes."

"Different drivers?"

"Yes, but they were always women."

"Did you recognize any of them?"

Henrietta Kingman whispered urgently to Davis, who stood as if to make an objection, but changed his mind and sat down, shaking his head.

"No," Goldberg said. "Usually I didn't see their faces clearly."

"Did he seem happy?"

Davis stood. "Objection! Asking for speculation!"

"Sustained," Judge Clarence said. "Rephrase the question."

"In your personal observation," O'Connor said, "was Mr. Jefferson a happy person?"

"Yes." Goldberg looked up at the courtroom ceiling, remembering. "He was always a cheerful guy, personality wise, his demeanor. When I think about seeing him at the office, passing in the hallway, running into each other at the garage, or sitting in meetings. Yes, I think of him as a happy guy."

"What about the times you saw him downstairs on the sidewalk?"

"When I saw him get out of those cars, usually he had the same happy smile on his face. But when he'd turn to go into the building, the smile always disappeared. Gone." Goldberg took a deep breath, exhaled loudly. "I don't know why I didn't pay more attention to this before. I should have spoken to him. I'll always regret not doing so."

For the first time since he sat at the witness stand, Goldberg looked at Thump.

As Davis rose to conduct his cross-examination, Henrietta Kingman clenched the sleeve of his jacket, pulled him down, and whispered in his ear, her face twisted in anger, her forefinger jabbing the air repeatedly in the direction of Goldberg on the witness stand. Davis nodded and moved away.

"Mr. Goldberg," Davis said, "professionally speaking, as an investment advisor, was the plaintiff different from other young professionals at KKG?"

"He was very aggressive. Driven."

"In what way?"

"One thing was that he made cold calls to prospects. KKG is not a firm where professionals normally engage in phone solicitations like this."

"What are the accepted business development methods at KKG?"

Goldberg smiled, a bit embarrassed. "There aren't any official methods. Our culture encourages dignified, subtle approach to marketing. We socialize with the right people, attend arts and theater events, charity galas, and so on. Clients come to us. We don't solicit them."

"Was he told to stop?"

Chuckling, Goldberg shook his head. "I teased him about it, but he didn't get the hint or, more likely, pretended not to get the hint."

"Do you receive phone solicitations from other businesses?"

"Like everyone else, I guess. Insurance salesmen, mortgage brokers, things like that."

"Would you do business with an insurance agent that cold-calls you to solicit your business?"

"No way." Goldberg laughed.

"Why not?"

"Obviously cold-calling is done by aggressive firms. It's cheap. Clearly they go for quantity rather than quality."

"Would you say that, in your opinion, prospective clients who had received solicitation calls from Mr. Jefferson were likely to have a similarly negative impression of KKG?"

"Perhaps."

"How could they not have a negative impression of KKG?"

"It's not so simple. I believe he chose prospects of high net worth, such as doctors and businesspeople, which made his approach more selective. I mean, if you get a call from a headhunter about a position with a top-notch international law firm, you don't think poorly of the headhunter just because she cold-called you, right?"

"I see your point," Davis said. "Did you report Mr. Jefferson's client solicitations to Mr. Kolbe or Miss Kingman?"

"No."

"Why?"

Goldberg hesitated. "There was an unspoken understanding that, well, we didn't judge Thump like everyone else. We had to be more forgiving toward him."

"Why?"

"Because he came from a different background."

"Didn't he come straight out of an MBA program?"

"He didn't actually finish the program, but that's beside the point." Goldberg raised a hand to stop Davis from asking another question. "It's not that he didn't have the education or the knowledge. Thump is a smart guy. But in our business, it's not just a matter of having the right credentials or technical ability. He didn't possess the social refinement that most of us have grown up with. We knew that he needed more time than others to learn how to function in our world, to become more attuned to our sophisticated environment, to develop—"

"Thank you," Davis interrupted him. "You've answered my question."

The jurors looked at each other, their expressions varying from bewilderment to disapproval.

Davis browsed his notes. "Were you and Mr. Jefferson on friendly terms?"

"Yes."

"And during those friendly five years of his employment with KKG, did he ever mentioned to you that he was being pressured for sex by any KKG partner or client?"

"No," Goldberg said. "He didn't."

"Not once?"

"No."

"Thank you!" Davis paused before the jury box, then returned to his seat.

Judge Clarence looked at O'Connor, who picked up her notes and rose for redirect.

"Mr. Goldberg, about the view from your window—"

"Yes?"

"That Friday afternoon, did you watch Mr. Jefferson exit the KKG building for the last time?"

After a long pause, Goldberg nodded. "Yes. I did."

The jurors leaned forward attentively.

"What did you see?"

"I saw him step out the front door of the building to the street with a cardboard box. He probably couldn't go through the back door connecting the lobby to the garage because he no longer had the cardkey."

"How did he look?"

"Confused. In shock. He put down the box and looked at the building."

"Did you see anyone else leave?"

"My partners usually leave early on Friday afternoons. I stayed to finish a couple of things."

"What happened then?"

Goldberg looked at Davis, but Davis kept his eyes down on his notes.

"Mr. Kolbe drove out, then Bo left. But when Henrietta's red Ferrari was leaving, Thump blocked her way. She got out of her car. He said something, she replied. I couldn't hear them."

"But you saw what happened next?"

"Yes," Goldberg said very quietly. "I did."

"Please describe what you saw."

"She pointed at the ground, and he went on his knees, pressing his hands under his chin, like in prayer."

A wave of murmuring rose from the audience, but quieted down within seconds.

"And then?"

"She bent over, said something which upset him terribly. He got up and yelled. She started going to her car. He stepped backward, tripped into the road, got hit. A homeless man ran over to help him."

"And Miss Kingman?"

"She drove away."

"And what did you do?"

"I called nine-one-one."

After the trial was adjourned for the day, O'Connor packed up her documents while Mrs. Jefferson came over to take Thump to the car.

"Don't forget," O'Connor said to Thump, "I need you at my office tonight to prepare for your testimony." She glanced at her watch. "Let's say seven thirty? It'll give you enough time for a quick dinner."

Jerald joined them, catching the last words, and said, "Why don't we eat together? There's a good Italian restaurant one block from our office."

"We don't need a restaurant," Mrs. Jefferson said. "My refrigerator is full, blessed be the good Lord. You two come over, and I'll put together a nice dinner for us." She didn't wait for their response, taking hold of the wheelchair and turning it toward the courtroom exit. "Come on now," she said. "Don't be shy."

O'Connor and Jerald looked at each other, uncertain.

Thump beckoned them to follow. "No point in arguing with her. Trust me on that."

CHAPTER 53

After dinner, O'Connor and Thump stayed seated at the table, now cleared of dishes, while Mrs. Jefferson changed into her hospital scrubs and prepared to leave for her night shift. Jerald was leaving with her, as she was giving him a ride home on her way to the hospital.

"Do good work," Mrs. Jefferson said. "There's hot water for tea in the kitchen. Help yourselves."

"Thanks, Mom. Good night."

Jerald blew a kiss to his wife from the door, and O'Connor replied more subtly, touching her finger to her lips and tilting it in his direction as the door closed.

"Let's start." O'Connor removed documents from a legal file. "We have a lot of ground to cover."

"Night shifts." Thump was still looking at the door. "I wish she didn't have to slave away like this."

"You'll be my wrap-up witness, the final evidentiary installment in our case, the last impression the jury will take with them."

"It's ironic, you know, because I was going to make her retire as soon as I became a partner—"

"It's crucial that we finish with a bang before Davis takes over and presents the defense case."

"If we win this case, I'll put money in an annuity account for her—"

"To win this case," O'Connor said with a hint of impatience, "you'll need to speak directly to the jurors from the witness stand, connect with them on a personal level. They want to hear from you, to get to know you, to understand who you really are."

"What about you?" Thump turned to her. "Don't the jury members need to understand who you really are?"

"It's your case," she said. "You're the plaintiff."

"And you're my lawyer."

"Your testimony is the key to the whole thing. We've got to prepare you for every possible—"

"You're avoiding my question." Thump reached over to a news rack and pulled out a folded newspaper. An article occupying multiple columns was circled with a red pen, and a few paragraphs were highlighted. He read from it: "*According to a colleague at the state court, Judge O'Connor had said: 'I'm tired of sending African American men to jail. Let's address the underlying cause: the black culture of victimhood, entitlement, and animosity toward whites. This culture creates a false justification for pathological social dysfunction and disregard for the law. Especially among young inner city African Americans, it's a culture of violence, drugs, rapes, and primal seed-spreading that results in countless out-of-wedlock children.' When confronted by a TV reporter, the former state judge was unrepentant, citing various statistics to support her prejudicial views that African Americans are disproportionally prone to crime and social dysfunction.*" Thump looked at her. "The jury members have read this also, I'm sure, and they want to hear your explanation. Are you a racist?"

O'Connor took the paper from his hand and put it away. "I'm not on trial, Mr. Jefferson."

"Neither am I."

"Actually, you are." She flipped through her yellow pad. "The jury will decide, and the choice they have is simple: either you were coerced into numerous sexual encounters or you were a whore, prostituting yourself for promotion and income."

"That's harsh."

"That's what your case boils down to." She held up her note pad. "Now, your testimony has to address the crucial—"

"It's your case too." Thump rested his hand on her forearm. "Come on, tell me, why did you take me on?"

"Why not?" She moved her arm away and exhaled. "It's my business now, taking on cases, trying to win and make money."

"You've expressed a very negative opinion of black men. Perhaps you haven't noticed, but I'm a black man."

"My opinion was that I was fed up seeing young black men come into my courtroom with rap sheets longer than the Bible. But I wish I had kept my mouth shut. You know why?"

"Because you lost your job."

"Because all I achieved was to get myself branded a racist. And I'm angry because what I said should have been said by African American leaders!" Her voice was rising. "Instead of whining about how white women cross the street if a black man approaches, or step out of the elevator when a black man enters, or lock their cars at the first sight of a black man coming down the sidewalk, instead of blaming white prejudice, black leaders should talk about the reasons for this fear."

"Easy for you to say." Thump pounded on his chest. "I've lived with these insults. Do you know how humiliating it is when white people give me that look, that quick appraising glance just before they decide how wide a circle they should take around me, as if I'm going to hit them or pull out a gun and rob them?"

"Why do you think they feel this way?"

"Prejudice. Racism. That's why!"

"Not for me. I'm not a racist."

"Then why are you afraid of black men?"

"I'm not going to discuss my personal feelings."

"Why not?"

"Don't bully me!"

Momentarily stunned, Thump held his hands up, showing her his palms. "Sorry. I didn't mean to—"

"It's fine." O'Connor thought for a moment. "Let me give you a benign example. You're driving a cute little convertible on a two-lane twisty road. First, in the opposite lane, you see a motorcycle approaching you. It doesn't bother you much, correct?"

Thump nodded.

"A moment later, a huge truck shows up ahead, barreling down the opposite lane toward you. It's a tractor trailer with six headlights and a cabin the size of a house. Now, even though this monster is still within its assigned lane, even though it has done nothing to indicate it's about to do anything to hurt you, still, at the very sight of it, you cringe, right?"

"Probably."

"Your chest tightens, your breathing quickens, and your hands grip the steering wheel. Am I right?"

"Yeah."

"See?" O'Connor used her hands to pantomime a scale. "You're discriminating. Here are two innocent drivers—one on his motorcycle, one in his tractor trailer—both drive their respective vehicles lawfully in the proper lane, neither have done anything to hurt you, yet you treat the truck driver as dangerous. You fear him."

"What's your point?"

"My point is that your mind and body react with fear because you associate the truck with higher risk. Your past experiences and knowledge cause your brain to signal that, compared with the motorcycle, a tractor trailer is more prone to taking wide turns and invading opposite lanes, more prone to sleepy drivers doing overtime, and more prone to causing devastation in the event of a collision. Similarly, white people know that a black man, statistically speaking, is much more likely to be dangerous. It's a fact."

"It's prejudice based on skin color."

"Because of the factual relation, that's all. No intelligent person would argue that there's causation here, that black skin is a cause for violent tendencies. Black skin is pigmentation, that's all."

"That's all? Just like that you wipe off all the history of white racism?"

"I don't care about the past. It was very sad. I'm so sorry you people experienced slavery, but this is now, today. Therefore there's a factual statistical connection, and hence the fearful association in people's minds between black skin and the risk of being the victim of a violent crime."

"You justify prejudice toward black people because of statistics? Don't you see how that's totally unfair to ninety percent of black people?"

"Who says life's supposed to be fair?" O'Connor shook her head. "I wish your community leaders—pastors, politicians, athletes—spent less time accusing whites of racism and more time accusing young black men of fueling racism by their behavior."

"You have no right to say that!"

"I agree, but someone has to say that it's unacceptable that every third black man is involved in crime. It's unacceptable that African American murder rates are five or ten times higher than whites—a hundred times higher in inner cities. It's unacceptable that so many black women have to raise kids without fathers, that multiple generations live on welfare and handouts. These things are unacceptable not only because they're morally wrong and socially destructive to African Americans' lives, but also because they pour oil on the flames of racism."

Thump turned his wheelchair and looked up at the portrait of Martin Luther King Jr. on the wall. "It's convenient to forget," he said, "that these problems didn't grow in a vacuum. Black people in America didn't develop high crime rates and broken families overnight."

"Don't give me the abuse excuse. I heard it too often in my courtroom."

"Call it what you want. Fact is, we African Americans experienced centuries of slavery, oppression, subjugation, segregation, then all the well-meaning, patronizing social programs that created dependency and self-loathing. These were like fertilizers that stimulated the criminal behavior and social dysfunction."

"It's a choice. Look at yourself. Didn't you come out all right?"

He laughed out loud.

"I'm serious," O'Connor said. "That's why I took your case. You studied hard and worked hard and got a bum deal despite all your efforts and diligence."

Thump started rolling his wheelchair across the room. "Come, I'll show you something."

O'Connor followed Thump down a short hallway to a door. He opened the door and rolled his wheelchair into a room. She entered behind him, and it took her breath away.

"I grew up in this room," he said.

Two of the walls were covered floor to ceiling in framed portraits of black men and women. The other two walls were covered with bookshelves, with the exception of a single window, which had a curtain with the logo of the Brooklyn Dodgers and the number *42*.

"Welcome to my childhood." Thump gestured at the portraits. "My mom used to buy these for me, one every week or two, and I had to memorize the achievements of the person before I earned the right to hang the picture up on my wall."

"Look at all of these people." O'Connor looked at the portraits. "This is incredible."

He pointed at a yellowish photo of a man in a white coat. "Do you recognize him?"

She shook her head.

"Dr. Charles R. Drew." Thump recited from memory. "Born June third, nineteen oh four. Died in a car accident on April first, nineteen fifty. He was a physician, a surgeon, and a scientist. He invented the original methods of blood transfusions, blood donations, and blood-plasma storage, which saved many thousands of soldiers in World War Two and formed the foundations for the American Red Cross blood bank. He once got fired after protesting racial segregation in blood donations."

"You still remember?"

"All of them. Scientists, entrepreneurs, writers, leaders, lawyers, artists, athletes." He pointed, rattling off the names. "Madame C.J. Walker, Booker T. Washington, Ralph Ellison, Alex Haley, Toni Morrison, Walter Mosley, Richard Wright, Jackie Robinson, Kareem Abdul-Jabbar, Muhammad Ali, Charles Barkley, Joe Louis, W.E.B. DuBois, James Meredith, Elijah Muhammad, Rosa Parks, Bobby Seale, Fred Shuttlesworth, Emmett Till, Walter White."

"Wait." O'Connor followed him along the rows of portraits. "I know them too." She pointed. "Halle Berry, Bill Cosby, Sammy Davis Jr., Morgan Freeman—I love him!—Gregory Hines, Lena Horne, James Earl Jones—love him too!—Spike Lee, Eddie Murphy,

Sidney Poitier, Richard Pryor, Will Smith, Denzel Washington, Oprah Winfrey."

"Very good," Thump said. "How about this line here?"

She looked up. "Thurgood Marshall—one of my heroes too—and, hum, I don't know this one."

"Kwesi Mfume, born October twenty—"

"Oh, the congressman!"

"And former president of the NAACP."

"He looks so young here." O'Connor peered at the photo. "He's a good example for young people, someone who turned his life around."

"At age twenty-three he quit crime, got a job, went to school." Thump chuckled. "My mom took me to meet him once at a local church where he was speaking."

O'Connor continued along, pointing. "This is Nelson Mandela, Jesse Jackson, Colin Powell, Clarence Thomas, Andrew Young, Louis Armstrong, Harry Belafonte, Chuck Berry, Ray Charles, Nat King Cole—we played his records at our wedding—Miles Davis, Duke Ellington, Aretha Franklin, Dizzy Gillespie, Jimi Hendrix, Billie Holiday, Michael Jackson, Diana Ross, and Stevie Wonder."

Thump laughed. "You sure know your black heroes. My mother would be pleased with you."

"That's good." O'Connor looked around. "Where's Barack Obama?"

"He's hanging in Mom's bedroom."

"Ah." She turned to the bookcases. "Did your mother make you read all of these books?"

"Most of them." He rolled over in his wheelchair and picked out a well-worn volume. "This one I had to memorize."

Taking it from him, O'Connor saw it was *Uncle Tom's Cabin.*

"This was my mom's main message." He took the book and placed it back on the shelf. "She kept saying, 'If you want to succeed in the white man's world, you must be an Uncle Tom.' That was her mantra, and it stuck."

"What did she mean?"

"She told me I had to be very strong, to build up all the strength it would take to make myself appear weak."

"Weak? In what way?"

"Be deferential, respectful, polite, no matter what. She used to tell me: 'If the white people piss on you, pretend it's rain.'"

They settled back at the dining room table. O'Connor spread her papers, her pen ready over the yellow pad. "I prepared a list of questions that I'm going to ask you, as well as a list of questions that Davis might ask you."

"You're very thorough."

"I try. But now, being here at your mother's place, it occurred to me that I neglected to predict one line of questioning Davis might pursue."

"What's that?"

"Family history. Specifically, he might ask about your father. Is he alive?"

"No," Thump said. "My father was killed in a gunfight when my mother was still pregnant with me. According to her, she was young, stupid, and in love, and he was handsome, clever, and deep into the heroin and cocaine business. That's all I know. His name is on my birth certificate—Torrance M. Jefferson—but otherwise he was not part of my life. Mom used to tell me," Thump imitated her voice, "*I don't want you to have any feelings for that man, lest you follow in his muddy footsteps away from the good Lord.*"

"She's quite a lady, your mom." O'Connor scribbled something and turned a page in her yellow pad.

"Yes, she is." Thump rolled his wheelchair to the adjoining living room and turned on the music, a rap song, at low volume.

"My questions," O'Connor said, "will be aimed at bolstering your image. Your answers will emphasize your hard work, success with colleagues and clients, and, in contrast, how Henrietta Kingman's actions held you down."

"This is a good song," Thump said. "Deep."

"On cross-examination, Davis will try to unravel the image I created. He'll probably start with your MBA grades and your failure to—"

"My mom was wrong, you know?" He nodded his head with the music, which was like a distant heartbeat, the lyrics vague. "I tried to be what she wanted me to be, and look where it got me."

"You must be ready," O'Connor said, "for Davis to try to box you in. He'll make you admit that you got into the MBA program on affirmative action."

"It's the big picture," Thump said, using a remote to increase the volume a bit. "The game is rigged, the cards are stacked against us."

"Davis will try to tie you up in knots." O'Connor browsed through her list. "Cause you to admit that you weren't good, that your actions proved your incompetence at KKG—"

"Listen." Thump rolled his wheelchair to the middle of the room and used the remote to raise the volume further. "Listen to the words."

The rap singer's voice emerged. "*Where you find them dealers, you will find them wheelers! Where you find them wheelers, you will find them pushers!*"

As the beating drums took over between the verses, O'Connor continued, raising her voice. "Davis will imply that you couldn't make it at KKG, that you had no talent, no real knowledge, so you used your dick to get ahead—"

"Here, listen to this." Thump's head rocked with the pace of the music. "Here it comes, the next line."

"*Cash n' carry, cash n' hurry, that will get them fok fok, that will get them fok fok! Cash n' hurry, cash n' bury, that will get them fok fok, that will get them fok fok!*"

"Did you hear the words?" Thump swayed back and forth. "It's the same, how they, the whites, the government, they made drugs illegal, which made them expensive, created temptation, irresistible for poor men with dreams."

"We have to prepare." O'Connor held up the documents. "It's important that you're ready for the questions—"

"Listen, here it comes again—"

"*Cash n' carry, cash n' hurry, that will get them fok fok, that will get them fok fok! Cash n' hurry, cash n' bury, that will get them fok fok, that will get them fok fok!*"

"You hear the double meaning?" Thump raised the volume again. "Drug money will get them sex, make them the alpha males, but it'll also get them screwed!"

The words came faster, more intense, and now the drumbeat, in between, was sharper, louder. He moved the wheels in opposite directions, swiveling the wheelchair around itself.

"Your answers will be critical," O'Connor said, her voice even louder. "You'll have to push back, to explain how you were good at business, at investments, how you're creative—"

"Creative niggers," Thump said, "smart niggers get into selling drugs to get money, status, the American dream, you understand? To get to be like the white man."

"*Them niggaz, go fok fok, ape it like them white fox, ape it like them white fox! Them white fox, go fok fok, niggaz under white fox, niggaz under white fox!*"

"Did you hear it?" Thump increased the volume further, the drumbeat now buzzing through the apartment. "That's the truth. Niggers want to, but never get to be white. Never."

O'Connor tried to speak again, but paused, watching him.

Thump rolled his wheelchair back and forth with the pace of the music, his eyes shut, his face turned up to the ceiling. "It's the dream, to be like white folks, to live like white folks, but they, they—" He paused, then cried, "No! Not *they*! *We! We* can never win this dream, this white freedom—"

"*Fok n' bury, carry bury, bury all them niggaz! Fok n' bury, hurry bury, bury all them niggaz! Fok n' bury, merry bury, bury all them niggaz!*"

Swaying, eyes shut, Thump's lips moved with the words.

"I'm going to leave the list of questions here." O'Connor left the yellow pad, collected all her other papers, and started for the door.

The music pace grew even faster, the volume louder.

"*Fok n' bury, carry bury, bury all them niggaz! Fok n' bury, hurry bury, bury all them niggaz! Fok n' bury, merry bury, bury all them niggaz!*"

O'Connor opened the door. She hesitated, looking at Thump, who was completely engrossed, as if in a trance, swaying, mouthing the words, tears flowing down his cheeks.

"*Bury merry, carry hurry, bury all them niggaz! Bury merry, carry hurry, bury all them niggaz! Bury merry, carry hurry, bury all them niggaz!*"

Stepping out, O'Connor closed the door behind her and paused. She listened through the door, then walked away, shaking her head, and went down the stairwell to her car.

When O'Connor got home, Jerald was already asleep. She tiptoed into their bedroom, slipped off her shoes and clothes, and crawled under the covers. She hugged him from behind, spooning him. He mumbled something and returned to sleep. She listened to his breathing, but in her head, the rap song kept playing, "*Bury merry, carry hurry, bury all them niggaz! Bury merry, carry hurry, bury all them niggaz! Bury merry, carry hurry, bury all them niggaz!*"

CHAPTER 54

Every seat in the courtroom was taken. Total silence accompanied Thump as he maneuvered the wheelchair to the witness stand and positioned it sideways, his casted leg pointing sideways. The courtroom deputy administered the oath.

"Mr. Jefferson." O'Connor approached with her yellow pad. "Five years ago, were you happy to join KKG?"

Thump took a deep breath. "Yes. I was very happy."

"Why?"

"Because of Mr. Kolbe. When I was still in school, I read an article about him in the *Baltimore Business Journal* and said to myself: I want to work with this man!"

At the defense table, Mr. Kolbe chuckled.

"Interesting," O'Connor said. "What impressed you so much?"

"First of all, he had a solid track record in choosing solid investments for his clients for the long term, and I wanted to learn from him."

"What about the large investment companies, like T. Rowe Price, Legg Mason, or Merrill Lynch? Wouldn't you rather work in a big corporation with a diversified work force than a small, white-shoe firm with a stuffy culture?"

"It's not easy to get hired by the large companies. I would have to come in as a personal assistant or even lower. I'd be just another guy among hundreds or even thousands of junior employees, no chance of working directly with a leader of Mr. Kolbe's caliber."

"Was there anything else about him that interested you?"

"He built KKG from nothing. That was a big thing for me, because I knew that my success also depended on me, and he would be sympathetic to it."

"And when you started working at KKG, did you remain an admirer of Mr. Kolbe?"

"Yes. He's a decisive leader, a natural with numbers, a gifted communicator, and a thoughtful strategist. And he's a gentlemen too."

"Wow." O'Connor chuckled. "Whose side are you on?"

Everyone laughed, including the jurors, who looked at Thump with respect for his honesty.

"How about Henrietta Kingman?"

Thump wiped sweat from his forehead. "She's very capable. But our relationship was different from the start."

"How so?"

"My first day at KKG, she locked the door and—" He lowered his eyes, his voice trailing off.

"And what?"

"She asked me if I knew how to please a woman."

"How did you answer?"

"I said that, yes, I do."

"And?"

"She asked me to show her."

"Did you?"

"Yes." His voice was down almost to a whisper. "I performed oral sex on her."

O'Connor turned slowly and looked at the defense table, where Kingman sat expressionless.

"Why did you do it?"

"She hired me. I was grateful."

"Did it happen again?"

"A couple of days later. Then it became a regular thing. Sometimes we progressed to full intercourse."

"In the office?"

"Yes."

"How often did you have sex?"

Thump glanced at O'Connor, then lowered his eyes again. "Whenever she wanted. And she supported my career. All the way."

"Did you ever go to her house?"

"No."

"Did she come to your place?"

"No."

"Did you go on vacations together?"

"No."

Kingman leaned over and whispered to Davis, shaking her head.

"Beside her," O'Connor said, "were there other women?"

"Not at first. But later, yes. She started asking me to help her with potential clients. Rich widows, businesswomen. Sometimes she gave my number to them and they would call me directly."

"Did you enjoy it?"

"They were very wealthy. I've never seen that kind of affluence, how these people lived—the cars, the homes, the servants, the jewelry. It was a way of life I very much wanted for myself."

"And the sex?"

He inhaled deeply. "It became part of the job. Some of them were very nice, others were, you know, a bit old."

"But you managed to do it?"

"Sex can be mechanical." He paused. "Talking about it now, it seems gross, at least in retrospect. But I didn't stop to ponder it, didn't analyze or agonize over it. Getting a job at KKG was an incredible opportunity, and having a partner like Miss Kingman in your corner is worth anything."

"Anything?"

He took a deep breath and exhaled loudly. "A condom is like a barrier between you and the other person. Doing it with Miss Kingman, or with these women, it was part of what I had to do to succeed."

"Did you feel abused?"

"Not at the time, no. Miss Kingman made me feel really special, like we had a secret deal that no one was aware of."

"How did she treat you?"

"She was warm and complimentary, always telling me how attractive I was, how my clothes were handsome. Also professionally, in business, she was very supportive. For me, because I wanted to become a partner one day, there was nothing better than having the number two partner in the firm helping me, opening doors for me, paving the way. It was too good to give up, even when the sex became too much—not just with her, but with the other women. It started to feel cheap."

O'Connor glanced at the jurors, whose faces were a mix of disgust and fascination.

"Did you ever try to discuss it with anyone else at KKG?"

"During my third year," Thump said. "I met a great girl, a schoolteacher, and I really liked her, wanted to pursue a serious relationship. I told Miss Kingman that it was time, you know, that I wanted to stop."

"What was her response?"

"She ignored what I said."

"What did you do?"

"I thought of speaking with Mr. Kolbe—discreetly, not to cause trouble."

"Why didn't you?"

"I was going to. We went sailing on the *Steady Hands* one Friday afternoon in the spring. Mr. Kolbe invited me, together with Mr. Goldberg and Mr. Chang. We sat in reclining chairs on the deck, cruising on the Chesapeake Bay, and Mr. Kolbe told a funny story about a client who hired an investigator to spy on his wife and found out she was paying an escort service. Mr. Kolbe said that the client was outraged at how much they charged to have sex with his old wife—and he was doing it with her for free!"

There were both laughs and groans in the courtroom.

"When I heard that," Thump said, "I realized how he would view what I was doing, and I also realized that he would be correct. What I was doing wasn't as bad as being a male escort, but it was similar."

"Do you regret spending five years like that?"

"No. I don't regret it. I *resent* it!" Thump's voice rose. "I resent being put in this position. I resent having to do it in order to achieve my dream, to be like Mr. Kolbe."

"Is it still your dream?"

"Yes. I love the business. You can actually do some good for people, help them realize their dreams." Thump looked down, his voice deflated. "All I wanted was to succeed at KKG. That's all I ever wanted."

The audience was mesmerized by this glimpse of his raw emotions. In the rear of the courtroom, sitting next to Mrs. Jefferson, Tiffany wiped tears.

"Nevertheless," O'Connor said quietly, "your dream didn't come true."

"Actually, it did come true." He looked up, taking a deep breath. "I had a great job with wonderful colleagues and a growing list of clients. And then I was promoted to VP. They actually made me an executive." Thump turned with effort to look at the defense table, where the KKG partners looked back at him. "And why not? I had done my share, earned my freedom." He tried to move his broken leg, and his face twisted in sudden pain.

"Tell us about the Boulder Trust presentation."

"Mr. Kolbe asked me to prepare it. It was my chance to cement my position at KKG by showing all of them—not only Miss Kingman—what a great investment manager I was." He paused, shaking his head. "But someone sabotaged me."

O'Connor handed him a glass of water, and he drank from it.

"I want to take you," she said, "to the day you were fired. When you left the building, what exactly happened?"

Closing his eyes, Thump took a moment to recall. "I stepped out the front door, carrying the box with my personal stuff, and suddenly felt very weak, so I put it down."

Thump dropped the box on the sidewalk. He looked up at the at the sign over the building entrance: *KKG Investment Management*

Inc. Higher up, the afternoon sun reflected in the windows, blinding him for a moment, and he shaded his eyes with his hand.

At the corner of the building, at the entry to the garage, the exit barrier rose. A dark-blue Rolls Royce emerged, Mr. Kolbe behind the wheel. Their eyes met, and Mr. Kolbe took advantage of a gap in traffic and drove off.

A moment later, Bo Chang drove out in his silver Aston Martin. Their eyes met, and Chang sped away.

Next, rumbling exhaust sounds came from the garage, the barrier came up again, and Henrietta Kingman drove out in her red Ferrari, the soft top open. She had to stop as traffic on Charles Street was busy and fast.

Thump ran over and blocked her way.

Kingman got out of the car, which remained idling across the sidewalk. She folded her arms on her chest, glaring at him.

"How?" Thump raised his arms in the air and dropped them. "How could you do this to me?"

"You made your bed," she said. "Now sleep in it and have nightmares."

Pointing at the building, Thump yelled, "This is my bed. My whole life!"

"Life is a barter. Give and take." She lowered her eyes and gazed at his crotch long enough to make a point. "Thump, or get thumped!"

He was shocked for a moment. "Fine. Take me back. I'll do what you want."

"Really?" She smirked. "Whatever I want?"

"Yes."

"Go down on your knees."

"What? Here?"

Kingman pointed at the ground. "Kneel! Beg! Beg me!"

Thump hesitated, then kneeled, hands pressed under his chin.

"Beg me, boy!"

"I beg you," he said. "Please take me back."

Bending closer to him, Kingman said, "Thump you!"

He was stunned.

"Did you hear me?" Kingman was yelling now. "Thump you! Thump you to hell!"

He got up slowly. "What kind of a monster are you?"

Done with him, Kingman headed back to her car.

"Answer me!" Thump walked backward, blocking her way. "Answer!"

She tried to get around him.

He kept stepping back, repeating, "Answer me!" His foot slipped at the sidewalk edge, and he tripped backward.

"That's all I remember," Thump said. "Next thing, I woke up in a hospital bed with tubes in my nose and arms and everywhere else. The doctors told me about the extent of surgeries done on my leg and hip."

O'Connor made a note in her pad. "How are you adjusting?"

"Physically, I manage. They're not sure about my hip, but the leg is healing. I hope to walk again, but some days it's hard to stay optimistic."

"And professionally?"

"It's been a nightmare." Thump wiped sweat from his forehead. "Without a letter of reference from KKG, everyone assumed I was fired for stealing or a similar offense. I can't get a job at another investment firm, and trying to build my own business, I've been unable to convince clients to sign up with me as an independent advisor. It's like professional leprosy."

"How do you handle this," O'Connor asked, "emotionally speaking?"

Thump struggled to answer. "I've always worked hard, always set concrete goals with specific strategies to meet them. I used to have so much fun achieving. Being alive!"

"And now?"

"Now I feel like I'm caught in a dark, suffocating limbo. I miss working, I miss my colleagues, I miss life. And worse than anything, I miss my fiancée."

On her way back to the plaintiff's table, O'Connor glanced at the audience, finding Tiffany, who was wiping tears with a tissue.

John W. Davis picked up on the subject while he was still getting up from his seat at the defense table.

"About your fiancée," Davis said, "after you vowed fidelity to her, you performed anal sex on another woman, correct?"

With effort, Thump said, "Yes."

"And this was your vanity plate." Davis held up a photo to show the jury. "*Thump!* It remained on your car until shortly before you left KKG, correct?"

"Yes."

"Were you promoting sexual prowess to colleagues? Strangers on the road?"

"No. It was just a nickname."

"Quite a nickname. And the rumors about your great genital size?"

"It was a joke. Started in college, perpetuated over the years. A joke."

"According to your complaint in this case, this joke helped you win clients and promotions. Is that correct?"

Thump didn't answer.

"That's the essence of your legal case here." Davis held up a bunch of papers. "Or is this lawsuit also a joke?"

Taking a deep breath, Thump sat back in the chair. "People believe what they want to believe."

"In other words, you used your sexual reputation for exceptional size to get ahead professionally and financially?"

"It wasn't my idea." He looked at Henrietta Kingman, sitting with her partners at the defense table. "I could have succeeded on merit."

"Is that so?" Davis turned and headed back to his seat. "I withdraw the question."

Judge Clarence peered over his reading glasses at O'Connor. "Do you have any questions in redirect, or shall we take a break?"

"Only one follow-up question." O'Connor stood and asked, "Mr. Jefferson, is your penis in fact exceptionally big?"

Davis jumped. "Objection! Prejudicial! Immaterial."

Her voice innocent, O'Connor said to the judge, "Your Honor, Mr. Davis opened the door by asking my client about his—and I quote—'*sexual reputation for exceptional size,*' as well as about his '*great genital size.*' These are Mr. Davis's own words. He can't object now to a follow-up question dealing precisely with the same specific subject matter."

"That's outrageous!" Davis approached the bench. "An assessment by Plaintiff of his own size is not evidence!"

"I agree," O'Connor said. "I'll rephrase my question."

"Thank you." Davis marched back toward the defense table.

"Mr. Jefferson," O'Connor said, "will you please lower your pants—"

The courtroom exploded, and O'Connor yelled the rest:

"—and show your penis to the jury so that they can judge your size for themselves?"

Judge Clarence pounded the gavel until order was restored.

Davis was back at the bench. "Objection!"

The judge looked at O'Connor. "This is a court of law, a trial, not a freak show."

"Indeed," she said, "this is a trial, but it's not just any trial. It's a trial dealing with a very specific set of circumstances that starts and ends with my client's sexuality or, more accurately, with the five years of sexual humiliation and servitude my client suffered at KKG. Besides, it is odd that my question, which calls for demonstrative evidentiary response, offends Mr. Davis's delicate sensitivities, while my genteel colleague himself did not shy away from spending the majority of his cross-examination on the very subject of my client's penis."

"Mr. Davis," the judge said, "you got us into a real mess here."

Davis stepped closer to the bench, pleading with the judge. "Your Honor, even if this is relevant as a follow up to my questions, you could rule it inadmissible as it is likely to cause the jury to feel undue sympathy with the plaintiff."

O'Connor sneered. "You're worried about sympathy? Should we hide his wheelchair too? This whole trial is about thumping! About his size! Let the jury members judge for themselves!"

Judge Clarence sat back, shaking his head. "I might have to allow this, perhaps by using medical experts, but it goes against every fiber in my judicial robe. Can you two somehow compromise?"

"Your Honor," Davis said, "I don't see how we can—"

"Ruth?" The judge looked at O'Connor. "The dignity of this court is at stake."

"Fine." She turned to Davis. "If you withdraw your objection to my previous question, I will drop the demand for physical viewing."

"Why would I agree?" Davis paused as he saw the judge's expression. "Upon further reflection, I withdraw my objection to the previous question, though I do so under protest."

"So noted." Judge Clarence turned to the court reporter. "Read the previous question from the record."

The court reporter read it. "*Mr. Jefferson, is your penis in fact exceptionally big?*"

Everyone looked at Thump, who seemed frozen in embarrassment and indecision.

"Go ahead," O'Connor said. "Answer in your own words."

"I've never measured it," Thump said. "I mean, I haven't used a ruler to compare it to others, but—"

"But what?"

"I don't think it's anything special," he said, glancing down. "Definitely since the accident, the wheelchair, the painkiller. Man, these days, it's practically dead."

There were a few awkward chuckles, but most of the audience was silent. Mrs. Jefferson put her arm around Tiffany, who shut her eyes and hung her head down.

At the defense table, Mr. Kolbe's face was red, Henrietta Kingman looked away, and Goldberg whispered, "Oh my God."

The fat black juror rolled her eyes. The Asian woman juror giggled, her hand sheltering her mouth. The old redneck looked down at his own crotch as if conducting a mental comparison.

CHAPTER 55

O'Connor and Jerald stopped at a diner on the way home. They ordered two salads and a single bowl of Maryland crab bisque to share.

"What's your feeling," Jerald asked, "as of now?"

"I don't know." O'Connor forked a piece of tomato. "It's not over yet. The defense is starting to present its evidence tomorrow. But Davis only asked for one day, which means he's confident that our case is very weak by itself."

"Surely you disagree, right?"

She shrugged.

"Tell me," he said. "If the jury had to decide based on our evidence only, what do you think they would have done?"

"All our evidence has been circumstantial." O'Connor ate the tomato. "It's a coin-toss case. He said, she said. And the burden of proof is on us as the plaintiff."

Jerald was taken aback. "You think we'd lose?"

She nodded.

"Well, you've done all you can."

"Thank you, dear, but it's too early for condolences. We could still win, but for that to happen, the defense has to screw up."

"You expect Davis to make a mistake?"

"There's a rotten fish at KKG." She took a spoonful from the soup bowl. "All I need is a hook, and I'll pull it out all the way into the open and stink up the whole courtroom."

Two elderly women at the next table were staring, and one of them asked, "Aren't you the lawyer in that juicy sex case?"

O'Connor nodded and spooned more soup.

"I thought so!"

"We saw you and him on TV," the other one said. "Such a handsome man, even in the wheelchair. No wonder all the women wanted him."

"It's not his looks they wanted," the other one said to her friend and turned back to O'Connor. "Please tell us. Is he really that big?"

"Ladies," Jerald said, "he's nothing compared to me."

The two women laughed. O'Connor rolled her eyes.

CHAPTER 56

In calling his first witness for the defense, John W. Davis went for a checkmate. The way Mr. Kolbe walked to the witness stand, his tall figure with broad shoulders and long arms, the perfect fit of his pressed suit and shined shoes, his gentlemanly manner with the courtroom deputy who administered the oath, the way he graciously smiled at the jurors as if saying *We're in this together.* All these subtle messages combined to communicate that he was above the fray, an elder statesman bearing decades of experience and wisdom—a man you could trust.

Watching this, Thump sipped water, his hand trembling.

"Mr. Kolbe," Davis said, "as founder of KKG, how do you feel about this case?"

Thinking for a moment, Mr. Kolbe said, "I feel deep sadness."

"What else."

"Revulsion." Then, with vigor, he added, "And disgust!"

Thump jerked back as if physically hit.

Davis nodded. "Why was Mr. Jefferson fired from KKG?"

"Because he embarrassed and damaged the firm by failing to prepare a strategic presentation for the annual meeting of the board of trustees of an incredibly important client—the Boulder Trust."

"For the record, was there any reason for firing Mr. Jefferson besides his failure with the key presentation?"

"No."

"What kind of an employee was he?"

"A nice kid. Likeable. Not the brightest, but smart enough. However, his performance was mediocre, from a professional and analytical point of assessment."

"Then why did KKG keep Mr. Jefferson for this long?"

"In my experience, having led a company for so many years, it's always about the employees. You invest your heart in the employees. They become like family." Mr. Kolbe chuckled as if embarrassed by the show of emotions. "As a result, it's very hard to let go, especially when you have invested time and energy in helping a young man, in guiding him, hoping he would let go of bad habits, of low standards of behavior and ethics."

"Why did it take five years to reach this conclusion?"

"He was a nice boy. People liked him, advocated for him, gave him chance after chance." Mr. Kolbe smiled gravely. "But there always comes a moment of truth, when the facts are too clear to ignore. We gave him a tremendously important assignment, and he failed. In fact, his error was too egregious that no one could argue that he should be forgiven, especially when he refused to take responsibility and continued to blame others. There's a limit, even to charity."

Several of the jurors actually nodded in agreement. Davis noticed and must have decided to quit while he was on top. "Thank you," he said. "No more questions."

"You're welcome," Mr. Kolbe said. "My pleasure."

O'Connor stood. "Mr. Kolbe, did you know what the nickname Thump stood for?"

"Nicknames are for young people." He chuckled. "Members of my generation address fellow professionals by their last name. Therefore, to me he was always Mr. Jefferson."

Thump sipped water, spilling some on his tie.

"Did you know," O'Connor continued, "that Mr. Jefferson was pleasuring Henrietta Kingman?"

"Yes."

Taken aback, O'Connor paused. "You did?"

"Yes," Mr. Kolbe said. "I knew she took enormous pleasure in mentoring him, helping him understand investment management, sharing her expertise and wisdom with him. Yes, I think Mr. Jefferson, as well as our other young professionals, have always given my colleague, Miss Kingman, a great deal of pleasure and pride when they achieved—"

"Sex, Mr. Kolbe. Did you know she was thumping him?"

His smile faded. He didn't answer.

"Did you know that Miss Kingman was having sex with a junior employee, a black man who's twenty-five years younger than her? Yes or no?"

"No, and I don't believe the accusations are true."

"Did you know that her clients were thumping him too?"

"No. These are falsehoods built upon falsehoods."

"How about potential clients? Did you know Miss Kingman frequently asked Mr. Jefferson to have sex with promising prospects?"

"I'll tell you what I do know." Mr. Kolbe's tone was no longer bemused. "I know that a former judge should be ashamed to ask such filthy, slanderous questions!"

"Answer the question please. Did you know that Miss Kingman used to send Mr. Jefferson to thump potential clients, that she pimped him to generate new business? Did you know?"

"I gave you my answer."

O'Connor looked at the judge.

"Mr. Kolbe," Judge Clarence said, "please answer the question."

"I didn't know," Mr. Kolbe said. "I couldn't know because none of it ever happened."

"Did you ever suspect that any sex, any at all, was going on at KKG?"

"People are people. They have urges, they do things, sometimes with unlikely partners. But no one at my firm aimed a loaded gun at him." He pointed a finger at Thump. "No one forced him to drop his pants!"

Thump grasped the table, breathing heavily.

"Am I to understand," O'Connor said, "that in your opinion, unless the boss points a loaded gun at the employee, or makes an explicit threat, there's no sexual harassment?"

"Correct." Mr. Kolbe glanced at Henrietta Kingman. "Consenting adults are free to do what they want, or not to do it if they don't want. It's called freedom of choice."

O'Connor followed his gaze. Without taking her eyes off Kingman, O'Connor said. "In other words, Mr. Kolbe, hypothetically, if you instructed your secretary to perform a sexual act for your pleasure, that would not constitute sexual harassment?"

Realizing that O'Connor was looking at her, Kingman's gaze shifted, and their eyes met.

"Mr. Kolbe," O'Connor said, still looking at Kingman. "Your answer?"

Seeing this, Davis stood up. "Objection! She's asking the witness to give a legal opinion about a hypothetical situation!"

"Sustained," Judge Clarence said. "Move on, Counselor."

"No problem." O'Connor pointed at Henrietta Kingman while slowly turning to face Mr. Kolbe. "Have you ever had a sexual relationship with your colleague, Miss Kingman?"

"Jesus Christ!" Davis threw down his pen. "Objection! I move for sanctions against opposing counsel!"

The judge looked at O'Connor. "You better have a good explanation for this new round of bomb throwing."

"I don't have an explanation," she said, "but I assure the court that this question is not, as Mr. Davis argues, hypothetical. It's also relevant and appropriate."

Judge Clarence sighed. "I'll take your word for it—for now. Objection overruled. Motion for sanctions denied. The witness will answer the question."

Mr. Kolbe looked as if he was about to explode, but in a fit of self-control, he took a deep breath, exhaled, turned to face the jury box, and said, "I did not have a sexual relationship with that woman, Miss Kingman."

"Your Honor," O'Connor said, facing the judge, "I'd like to call an impeachment witness, then resume my cross-examination of this witness."

"I see," Judge Clarence said. "Who do you wish to call?"

"I call Henrietta Kingman to the stand."

Kingman glared at Davis, but he didn't object.

CHAPTER 57

With the full courtroom watching in silence, Kingman went to the witness stand. Her bearing was proud as usual, but her lips were pressed together tightly as she sat down.

"Miss Kingman," Judge Clarence said, "I'd like to remind you that you're still under oath."

She nodded.

O'Connor approached the witness stand. "Let me say something before we start." Her voice was uncharacteristically gentle. "I'd like to preface this examination by apologizing for having to pursue this subject of the relationship between Mr. Kolbe and you. Sadly, with sexual wrongdoing, victims are often more ashamed than their abusers."

"Spare me." Kingman's voice was painfully hoarse, and she cleared her throat before adding, "How would you know?"

"I do," O'Connor said. "From personal experience."

The two women looked at each other, and after a long moment, Kingman gestured as if saying, "Go ahead."

"Earlier in this trial," O'Connor said, "you testified that you worked at the firm for a long time until Mr. Kolbe made you a partner, correct?"

"Yes. I've been at the firm for a total of twenty-seven years, the last seven as a partner."

"And Mr. Kolbe announced your promotion to partner at a firm picnic, is that right?"

"Yes."

"More specifically, it was the annual Fourth of July picnic, seven years ago, correct?"

"Yes."

"It must have been the most delightful picnic ever, yes?"

After a brief hesitation, Kingman nodded. "Becoming a partner was the realization of a lifelong aspiration." She paused. "But to be perfectly accurate, I did not actually attend that annual picnic."

"Why not?"

"A brief hospitalization. I was back at the office within a few days."

"Was that hospitalization related to your throat condition?"

Kingman nodded, but Davis said, "Objection! Medical privacy!"

"I believe," O'Connor said, "that the witness has already answered affirmatively by nodding her head."

Judge Clarence turned to Kingman.

"I did," she said. "The answer is yes."

"Nevertheless," Davis insisted, "I'd like to maintain my objection to any further questions dealing with Miss Kingman's medical history, which is totally irrelevant to this case."

The judge looked at O'Connor. "Counselor?"

"It's relevant," she said. "You have my word."

"I'll allow you to proceed," Judge Clarence said. "But if it turns out that this line of questioning does not lead to relevant evidence, I'll impose sanctions. Is that clear?"

"Yes, Your Honor." O'Connor picked up a sheet of paper from the table. "Miss Kingman, according to records maintained by the City of Baltimore, seven years ago, on July third, an ambulance was called to KKG offices for a choking incident. The patient, according to the report, was a female in her late forties. Was it you?"

The expression on Kingman's face transformed from the guarded confidence of a powerful woman to abject fear. She didn't answer.

"Miss Kingman?" O'Connor came closer, but not in a threatening way. "I'm sorry, but you'll have to answer."

Kingman coughed. "Yes. It was me."

"Please describe the circumstances."

Kingman looked at Mr. Kolbe.

He shook his head.

O'Connor took a few steps aside, repositioning herself so that she blocked their view of each other. "Please, Miss Kingman. Go ahead. Tell us what happened that caused you to choke on July third, seven years ago."

At the defense table, Mr. Kolbe said something to Davis, who got up. But before he could say anything, Judge Clarence motioned him to sit down.

"I was in his office," Kingman said, pointing at Mr. Kolbe. "We had just come back from lunch, and I asked him when he was going to make me a partner."

"Go ahead," O'Connor said. "Tell us what happened."

CHAPTER 58

They stood on the Persian rug in the middle of his large office, facing each other. Mr. Kolbe reached and touched the ruby hairpin that held Kingman's hair together.

"Henrietta," he said, "don't you trust me?"

She straightened his tie. "I do. Of course I do."

"Good." He slowly pulled out the pin, releasing her carrot-colored hair, which cascaded in thick locks over her shoulders. "This is beautiful."

She looked up at him. "You promised that I'd be a partner by January. It's July already."

He combed her hair with his hands, admiring it. "Have patience. All in good time."

"I just want to know when."

"Soon. Trust me." Mr. Kolbe put his hands on her shoulders. "I'll take care of you, like always."

"But when?"

"Soon." He pressed down on her shoulders. "But right now, you got to take care of me."

"Soon?" Kingman knelt in front of him, still looking up at his face. "How soon?"

"Very soon."

"It's not fair." She unbuckled his belt. "We've been having sex for—"

"This isn't sex. It's a little fun, that's all."

Kingman unzipped him and reached inside. "Whatever you call it, I've served you for twenty years, paid my dues."

"Sure. Sure." Mr. Kolbe collected her hair in his hands, clasping it tightly. "You're doing great. The best."

Kingman pulled his erect penis out. "I deserve partnership."

"You'll get what you deserve. Don't worry."

"I'm ready for it." She rubbed him with her hand.

He groaned with pleasure. "That's my girl."

"My partner." She rubbed him harder, his crown aimed at her lips. "Now you try to say it: my partner. My pah—"

"Pah!" Mr. Kolbe shoved his penis into her mouth, silencing her. "Here's your pah!"

She moaned, but didn't resist.

"Pah!" He thrust in, and again. "Pah! Pah! Pah!"

She tried to pull back, but he was holding her hair tightly.

"Pah! Pah! Pah!" Mr. Kolbe's pace grew faster. "Pah! Pah! Pah!"

Kingman made gagging sounds, which seemed to excite him. He pounded hard, all the way to the back of her mouth. She tried to push him away, and he let go with one hand, collected a fistful of her hair, and clenched his fingers on it, holding on, going even harder, deeper.

Kingman moaned and gagged, and then she started to heave. But he wasn't looking down at her anymore, his eyes glazed over, aimed forward, unfocused as he pounded away, approaching climax. She struggled, panicked, but she was too small and he was holding too tightly.

She retched, and vomit shot up from her stomach. It had nowhere to go but into her lungs, and she literally drowned in it without him even noticing as he reached climax and came with a few last powerful thrusts and a deep groan.

CHAPTER 59

The courtroom was in collective shock as Kingman reached for a glass of water. She drank from it continuously until she emptied it. Then she put it down, dabbed her lips with a napkin, and cleared her throat.

"When the medics arrived," she said, "I wasn't breathing. They had to suction my airways and lungs very quickly. They pushed a tube in, probably a size too big for someone small like me. It damaged my vocal cords. They had no choice—I was dying. And they brought me back, so I'm thankful."

"Of course," O'Connor said. "Did they take you to the hospital?"

"Yes."

"Did Mr. Kolbe accompany you?"

"No. He went to meet John." She pointed at Davis.

"And then?"

"He made me a full partner the next day and renamed the firm. It became the Kolbe Kingman Group—in short, KKG."

"And two years later, you hired Mr. Jefferson, and history repeated itself?"

Kingman seemed surprised by the suggestion. "That's not true. As I told you before, when you asked: I never pressured him to have sex."

"But you did have sex with him?"

"Consensual. You never asked me about that."

"I'm asking now."

"We had an intimate relationship. We're both adults. We both enjoyed it."

"Do you actually believe that was the case?"

"He's a man. There's no faking with men. He was as excited as I was."

"Really?"

"Yes. I know he enjoyed it as much as I did. It was totally mutual."

"Mutual?" O'Connor waved toward Thump. "A black man, twenty-five years younger than you?"

"So what? How many men sleep with women half their age?" Kingman was defiant. "I'm in good shape, I'm successful, and I had a lot to offer him."

"Didn't his career depend on you?"

"There was no dependency. We helped each other in different ways."

"Professionally, didn't he owe you everything—past, present, and future?"

"I advocated for him. What's wrong with that?" Kingman was getting angry. "He'd soon be a partner if not for his betrayal!"

The jurors looked at each other, their expressions ranging from shock to confusion.

CHAPTER 60

When Mr. Kolbe returned to the witness stand, his easy manner had stiffened and his face had tensed up, but he still had the imposing presence of a powerful lion perched proudly above it all.

"Do you realize," O'Connor asked, "how the pattern of sexual harassment started with you?"

"There was never any harassment."

"You heard Miss Kingman's testimony. Was she lying?"

"I won't discuss private matters."

Judge Clarence didn't wait for O'Connor to seek help. "Mr. Kolbe, when you hear a question, you must answer it."

"Let me repeat the question," O'Connor said. "Was Miss Kingman lying about what happened that July third in your office?"

"Lying?" Mr. Kolbe glanced at Kingman. "I don't know. My own recollection of that day is totally different, but this might be a subjective impression."

"Whatever the details were, in terms of the big picture, what she described—being pressured by her boss to engage in sexual activity—is awfully similar to what happened to my client. I think we have a pattern of harassment, don't you agree?"

"No."

"Why is this case different than your relationship with Miss Kingman?"

"There's no similarity." He sneered. "You compare Henrietta Kingman to your client?"

Thump breathed hard. He loosened his tie and undid the top button of his shirt.

"At the time, she was an employee who was dependent on her boss for her livelihood and future career. Was it not the same with Mr. Jefferson, several years later, depending on Miss Kingman for his career while she played the role of the abusive boss?"

"You want me to tell you the difference?" He pointed toward Kingman. "Henrietta is a competent, honest woman who earned her position with talent and dedication. But your client?" He pointed at Thump. "There's an incompetent, slick prick who slithered through the cracks into my firm, took advantage of an older woman in the office, used her emotional vulnerability to manipulate her, to get her to help him and protect him. But he failed at his job, got fired, and now he's trying to extort money by dragging us through the mud with personal matters that are nobody's business!"

Thump's eyelids fluttered, and he struggled to stay focused.

"Level with us, Mr. Kolbe." O'Connor stepped closer to the witness stand. "On that Friday, didn't you and Miss Kingman discuss Mr. Jefferson's refusal to continue thumping Sharon Boulder, front or rear?"

"No!"

"Didn't you discuss his years of thumping Kingman herself?"

"No, goddamn it!"

Thump swayed in his wheelchair.

From behind, Tiffany noticed something was amiss and tried to see what was wrong with him.

O'Connor stepped even closer to Mr. Kolbe. "Didn't you guys make a hasty decision to fire him quickly, get rid of an embarrassing reminder of your own dirty secrets?"

"No!" Mr. Kolbe hit his fist on the railing. "No! No! No!"

Thump's eyes rolled back, but he recovered, managing to stay up.

"Didn't you say to each other," O'Connor said, now very close, practically in Mr. Kolbe's face, "what the hell, thump that nigger boy!"

"Lies! All lies!" Mr. Kolbe pointed at Thump. "Look at him! We pulled him from the gutter that spawned him and brought him into civilization!" Losing restraint, Mr. Kolbe was yelling now. "That was our mistake! We treated him better than his kind deserves! And what's our reward? He brought the gutter to us! Turned my firm into a street corner, pimped himself to our clients—"

With an audible groan, Thump collapsed, falling out of his wheelchair to the floor, his arms open wide, his mouth gaping.

Panic broke out in the courtroom.

CHAPTER 61

O'Connor spent the bulk of her closing arguments before the jury on recounting Thump's history at KKG, the circumstances of his firing, and the evidence supporting his version of events.

"In summary," she said, "please remember that sexual harassment is rarely clear cut. There are no video recordings that show us exactly what happened. Rather, we have to infer from the totality of the evidence, from the words and manner of the witnesses, from related facts and patterns of behavior, and from motives."

O'Connor turned from the jury and gestured toward the KKG partners at the defense table.

"Sexual harassment," she said, "can happen politely, perpetrated by well-dressed professionals in well-appointed offices and without a single harsh word. Those with power don't have to raise their voice or make explicit demands. The raised stick and dangling carrot are as real as your next paycheck and your next promotion."

She then gestured at the vacant plaintiff's table, where Thump had sat.

"Victims often cooperate to keep their jobs, or even go along with a relationship for years in order to protect their careers and chances of promotion. But the length of time and the appearance of consent do not change the fact that they are in a position of weakness, that they are coerced by professional vulnerability and dependency, and that they suffer. And when careers are ruined, lives are destroyed, and hearts are broken, it is up to you, and only up to you, each and every one of you." She held her hands out to them. "You, a jury of our peers, you have the power to uphold the law, deliver justice, and restore fairness. Don't be afraid."

Davis similarly did his best to offer a succinct review of the evidence from his clients' point of view. After going into great detail, he put aside his notes and approached the jury box.

"Look," he said, "I know how hard it is to know what really happened between people. But you must realize that there is no hard evidence to support the contention that anyone forced the plaintiff to do anything he didn't want to do. In fact, the most striking evidence is the lack of it. Remember, as you deliberate about this case, that not one of his friends at KKG ever heard Mr. Jefferson complain about any of the unsavory events that he suddenly brought up in this complaint—after he was fired for a real and undisputed failure at a crucial assignment."

He turned and waved at O'Connor, sitting alone at the plaintiff's table.

"They were supposed to meet the burden of proof. They were supposed to prove to you, with real evidence, that it was more likely than not that sexual harassment took place. But they failed."

Facing the jury, he sighed. "Beside the legalese and hype, the plaintiff threw a lot of mud across this courtroom in the past few days. I'm sure you feel as soiled as I feel."

He shook his head for a long moment.

"Now, let us admit to each other that we all feel bad about Mr. Jefferson's recent medical crisis. We're all human, and we're conditioned to feel sympathy for another person who's undoubtedly experiencing misfortune. But your decision here cannot be based on sympathies or emotions. You must decide based on the actual evidence presented to you. And what is the basic fact of this case, a fact even they don't dispute?"

Pausing, he looked from face to face.

"There is no dispute that it was the plaintiff, Mr. Jefferson who proclaimed his sexual prowess and, by doing so, seduced his targets. He himself was the driving force behind his myriad erotic escapades—real or imagined. Therefore, he has no right to complain, and you should deny him any remedy in this smutty, immoral attack on the honorable firm of KKG Investment Management Inc."

CHAPTER 62

Judge Clarence gave his instructions to the jury, explaining how they should discuss the evidence, maintain total secrecy, and in the end take a vote on each of the causes of action: Sexual Harassment, Negligent Personal Injury, and Intentional Infliction of Emotional Distress. Then he sent them home to get a good night's sleep before starting deliberations the next morning.

O'Connor headed straight to the hospital. She found Mrs. Jefferson and Tiffany on a bench in the waiting room outside the ICU. They hugged her.

"It was an embolism." Tiffany's eyes were red and glistening.

"As the Lord is my witness," Mrs. Jefferson said, "I told him it would happen if he didn't move around. I told him!"

Tiffany smiled sadly. "It's not his fault. These things happen after major injuries. Blood clots form somewhere in the body, then a piece breaks off and travels to the lungs."

"We almost lost him." Mrs. Jefferson sniffled. "A close call."

They sat together on the bench.

"It's a close call at court too." O'Connor held a finger and a thumb close together. "Can go either way."

Tiffany blew her nose into a tissue. "Any indications from the jury?"

"Too early," O'Connor said. "They gave us the poker face treatment during closing arguments. Deliberations start tomorrow."

"For how long?"

"No way to know. A day, a week, or they might come out by unchtime tomorrow with a verdict." O'Connor glanced at the closed ICU doors. “It seems unimportant now. What do the doctors say?”

“What can they say?” Mrs. Jefferson sighed. “They’ll keep him in intensive care overnight, and then we’ll see.”

CHAPTER 63

In the jury room, the jurors settled at a rectangular conference table, falling into an unspoken divide: the black jurors sat on one side, the whites on the other, and the Asian woman sat at the head of the table, wielding a pen and a yellow pad.

"Good morning everybody." She wrote her name at the top. "I am Lin. We already know each other a little bit, but now we start to work. You say your names, and I take notes."

The young black man said, "I'm Abdul."

The fat black woman said, "Shawna."

The old black woman with big glasses was next. "Miss Hill."

"What?" Shawna looked at her. "No first name?"

"Thirty-five years teaching middle school," Miss Hill said. "Even my husband has to call me Miss Hill, or he gets no dinner."

"That's cool." The young white woman with tattoos dropped a cigarette pack on the table. "I'm Danielle. No Miss."

The old redneck said, "You can call me Big Joe."

"Big Joe?" Lin smiled and covered her mouth.

"That's right," he said. "Enough with the fussing. Let's start discussing the issues already."

"Like what?" Abdul looked around the table. "It's totally simple. The black dude got screwed."

"We're doing rhymes?" Shawna raised her hand. "I got one: the brother got clobber!"

"Clobbered," Miss Hill said. "Past tense requires *ED* at the end of the verb. But you could try this: the brother got farther by humpin' the pumpkin."

Shawna and Danielle booed and laughed while Lin shook her head, struggling not to laugh.

"Let me try," Abdul said. "*A hunk named Thump, who … humped and bumped … was dumped after he flunked—*"

"What is this?" Big Joe sat back, hands folded over his belly. "Black poetry night first thing in the morning?"

"Everything is good," Lin gestured for calm. "No problem. We now discuss first claim." She looked at her notes. "If there was sexual harassment."

"When?" Abdul held his hands apart. "There are two different time periods. The long stretch of employment from when he was hired until he got engaged, and then the last few days."

"You can't slice it into sections," Shawna said. "It's not a sausage. Didn't you hear? Five years ago, when he started, that Kingman woman put him on his knees and gave him a mouthful of her honeydew. If that's not sexual harassment then I'm a skinny blond chick from Bel Air, right?"

"Wow," Abdul said. "Great costume!"

"What harassment?" Big Joe waved his hand dismissively. "The guy marketed himself as Thump, armed and ready for action. Hire me and I'll be your personal thumping toy. How can you blame her?"

"Children use nicknames," Miss Hill said. "It's a thing they do, boys in particular."

"His nickname was a sexual advertisement. Plain and simple."

"His nickname," Shawna said, "wasn't an invitation for a rich white bitch to extort sexual services from him in exchange for the opportunity to work hard and succeed in the company."

"Give me a break," Big Joe said. "What else could this nickname imply? He's called Thump because he's good at clapping hands? Hammering nails into wood? Please! Be honest! When you hear it—Thump!—you think of his prick. Don't deny it."

"*You* think of his prick!" Shawna's voice was rising. "Because he's a black man, that's why. Even if he didn't have a nickname you'd still think of it, you'd still think of how big it must be."

Big Joe snorted. "Why would I think that?"

"Because when you white boys look at black men, you experience penis envy. That's why."

"That's a bunch of crap."

"Is it? Then let me ask you this: When you meet a white guy whose nicknamed is Dick, do you think of his penis? Do you assume he's promoting himself as 'armed and ready for action' with an extra-large dick? Do you support employers' right to force white Dicks into sex, or does this rule only work against black dudes?"

"You have a chip on your shoulder," Big Joe said. "White, black, I don't care. Didn't you hear the evidence? The guy pranced around with an explicit nickname before he was even hired. Thump was his brand!"

"Pardon me," Danielle said, "but everyone in that hoity-toity company had dirty nicknames. And what's with that big boss, Kolbe, who by the way reminds me of my ex-father-in-law, another pompous fart who couldn't keep his slimy hands off my butt. He made his secretary blow him for years."

"Who?" Shawna looked at her. "Your ex-father-in-law?"

"No! That Kolbe guy, when Kingman was his secretary."

"Oh, right. Hey, that whole office was a shitty place to work, if you ask me."

Abdul laughed. "Only if you don't know how to have fun."

"Shush, you!" Shawna threw candy at him. "Bad boy!"

Lin knuckled the table. "Please, please. The judge said we should decide if that place was a 'hostile work environment.' Was it?"

"Not for the partners," Shawna said. "But for a hot black stud it was hostile, no question about it."

"I agree," Danielle said.

"I'll tell you something," Big Joe said. "You have no idea how these rich people are, how they see everyone else. They pay the bills, the salaries, so they're entitled to do whatever they want. It's capitalism, folks! That's your problem—you just don't understand rich people."

Miss Hill peered at him through her thick glasses. "And you do?"

"I drove a limo in this city for thirty years. You learn a lot sitting quietly at the steering wheel, listening to your passengers, watching what they do in the backseat." Big Joe shook his head. "I've seen it all, and I can tell you that these big money people, they're not like you and me. They don't give a flying brick what little people like us think about them, because if not for them, we'd be starving to death. These people, they work hard, they play hard, and they screw hard—in business and in the ass."

"Ouch." Shawna made a face. "Only there? No other orifices?"

"What's that?" Lin looked around the table. "I don't know that word."

"Orifice," Miss Hill said. "Noun. Body cavity. Hole."

"Uh." Lin covered her mouth, blushing. "Sorry."

Abdul burst out laughing, and the others joined him.

CHAPTER 64

Ruth O'Connor spent the morning at her office, catching up on mail and bills. She was sitting at her desk when she heard a voice from the door.

"Hi there." John W. Davis came in. "Sorry to barge in like this, but your secretary isn't at her desk."

"I don't have a secretary." She gestured at a chair across the desk. "Jerald helps me when I need it."

Davis looked closely at the framed certificates on the credenza, one from St. Mary's College, the other from Yale Law School. "Good education has its advantages, doesn't it?"

"It depends."

"True, there are exceptions to every rule." He sat down, pleased with himself. "You did a superb job at the trial. We were all very impressed."

"Thank you."

"Too bad about the facts, though. Preponderance of the evidence clearly tips against your client."

"That's for the jury to decide."

"And they will decide for KKG, we are confident. And not for lack of effort—you did everything possible for your client. I hope he appreciates it."

"He does."

"Cozy little place you got here." Davis looked around the modest office. "You know, with your background, your experience and analytical skills, you would be a great asset to any major law firm. Why waste your time and talent on lousy cases for lame clients when you could serve deep-pocket corporations? My firm would be very interested—"

"You're not here to offer me a job, are you?"

He chuckled. "No."

"How much are they offering?"

"It wasn't easy. Dan Kolbe was furious with all that unnecessary airing out all that embarrassing history about—"

"How much?"

"Look, I managed to convince them that this boy, his condition, poor chap, he's already been punished enough."

O'Connor raised her hand. "John, get to the point. How much?"

"Out of compassion," Davis said, "not because of any fault or wrongdoing, KKG is offering to pay him a severance bonus equal to six months' salary. We'll throw in a bit more for medical expenses, for humanitarian reasons. But the whole thing will remain confidential, and he has to withdraw all his claims. That's a must—he'll submit a motion asking Judge Clarence to dismiss the case with prejudice. This part is nonnegotiable."

"Thanks for the offer. I'll let him know."

Davis looked at her, surprised. "That's it?"

"It's his decision."

"Technically, yes, but it's really up to you, as his counsel. You should advise him to accept it. I'm sure he'll follow your recommendation."

"I can't recommend it."

"Why?"

"My client has a lot at stake here, and it's not all about money."

"What else is there but money?"

"His career. His reputation." She shrugged. "His self-respect, I guess."

Davis considered it for a moment. "I can't promise anything, but I might be able to convince KKG to give him a basic letter of reference, confirming that he left the firm in good repute, or in good standing, something like that."

"That's nice," O'Connor said. "But after all the publicity in this case, I doubt there's any value to a—what did you call it?—*basic letter of reference.*"

"As they say, beggars can't be choosers." Davis rubbed his hands. "It's a good offer. A fair settlement. Will you convince him to accept it?"

"I won't pressure him one way or another."

Davis pursed his lips. "That's too bad."

"I'll let you know his decision by tomorrow."

"That's not good enough." Davis drew a piece of paper from the inside pocket of his jacket. "I wanted to avoid this, but you leave me no choice."

O'Connor held the paper and read it:

St. Mary's Trumpet
October 21, 1982

Rape Investigation Update: Police suspended their investigation of four African American football players suspected of gang-rape, citing lack of cooperation from the unnamed victim, a Caucasian student who has since recovered from her injuries, graduated from St. Mary's and went on to attend law school.

"What I find fascinating," Davis said, "is the fact that, more often than not, our racial views are rooted in personal experiences."

O'Connor's hands shook as she put the sheet of paper down on her desk.

"I'm truly sorry, Ruth. All they want is to close the door on this ugly case. Your client would be well served by accepting this settlement. It's in everybody's interest."

"Not in my client's interest."

"His interest?" Davis sneered. "My God, did he really think he could beat a powerful firm like KKG? Who does he think he is?"

"That's exactly what this case is about." She stood.

Davis also got up, facing her across the desk. "He has to accept the settlement."

"And if he doesn't, your clients will make sure this piece of old news comes out?"

He gestured to indicate it was out of his hands.

O'Connor crumpled the piece of paper into a ball. "My client, a proud young man, submitted himself to awful public humiliation in pursuit of justice. Right now he's in the hospital, fighting for his life. And you think that I'd betray his trust in me to keep my youthful indiscretion a secret?"

"It's hardly a matter of youthful indiscretion. You refused to help police, you prevented law enforcement from prosecuting four rapists. Who knows how many more women those animals went on to rape?"

"None."

Davis laughed. "How in the world do you know that?"

"I do." O'Connor pulled open a filing drawer and took out a thick folder. "One is a legal aid counsel in Virginia, married with three children, now grown. Another went on to play football professionally and, upon retirement, volunteered to coach a youth league in rural Georgia. He and his wife raised four sons. The third became a dentist, married a schoolteacher, raised one daughter, and lost his wife to cancer last year."

"There were four, no?"

"The fourth joined the navy after graduating from St. Mary's. He died in the first Iraq war. Do you want to see a copy of his Purple Heart citation?"

"You kept tabs on the men who raped you?"

"I let those boys off, but I passed a message to them through a friend that if any one of them ever screwed up, I'd blow this whole thing up and destroy them all. That way, each one of them knew that if he tripped, they would all fall. And it worked."

"But why did you let them off? How could you take a risk that other girls would be attacked?"

"Because it wasn't all their fault. I was young, attractive and careless. I went drinking with them, joined them for more drinking in their frat house. When I realized, through the stupor of alcohol, that they had taken off their clothes, I started fighting which they misinterpreted as playing hard to get. Things go rough, and rougher, and then really bad. We were all very drunk, and I passed out. They were big guys, drunk and totally turned on, and they wrecked me, though I don't think they meant to do that. Destroying their lives would have been unfair, and there was no way to punish them in a lesser way."

"I appreciate you sharing this with me, I do." Davis sighed. "But my clients only care about one thing. Mr. Jefferson must accept the settlement and dismiss his case. Otherwise they will leak this story, Ruth. I know they will and I know it will destroy you. Is it really worth it to you?"

"I can take it. Problem is, even though this story is old, it's about sex, violence, and race. There's going to be a media frenzy." O'Connor rested her hand on the file. "Any half-ass reporter could make some calls to classmates of ours at St. Mary's, figure out who the four football players were, and dig up this information. Their families would be ruined."

"Old sins come back to haunt the guilty. It rings of biblical justice, don't you think?"

She put the file back in the drawer. "It rings of extortion to me."

Davis shrugged. "I'm only a messenger."

"I'll tell you what you are." O'Connor threw the crumpled paper across the desk. "A whore, that's what you are. An expensive whore."

CHAPTER 65

The courtroom deputy knocked on the door and entered the jury deliberation room carrying two large paper bags with Chinese takeout containers. He handed out the individual orders and left. The jurors brought their loaded plates to the table and sat down to continue discussing the case while eating.

Lin rolled noodles onto her chopsticks. "What about the last week, after he refused to do it anymore? That would be harassment." She slurped the noodles into her mouth.

"And then," Abdul said, "she fired him."

"Incorrect," Miss Hill said. "She didn't fire him. The company fired him."

"You really think so?" Shawna dipped a spring roll in a sauce cup. "Kingman was his mentor. She got him all the promotions, right? No one denied that. Now, if she's behind all his promotions, what makes you think she's not the one who bit off his head?" With that, Shawna bit off half the spring roll.

Big Joe held up a piece of orange chicken. "Are you surprised? For five years, no problem, no complaints, he's thumping that Hot Damn redhead gal—"

"Phew!" Abdul made a face. "She's way too old. Skinny too!"

Miss Hill peered at him over her Styrofoam bowl of soup. "What do you have against old and skinny?"

"Doesn't matter," Big Joe said. "He probably shut his eyes and fantasized he's thumping Beyoncé."

"Hey!" Shawna pointed at him with the spring roll, its chomped end dipped in red sauce. "That's a racist comment. You're just like that Kolbe boss." She imitated him. "*We pulled him from the gutter that spawned him and brought him into civilization! Better than his kind deserves!*"

"I stand corrected," Big Joe said. "Forget Beyoncé. Let's say he imagined he was thumping Julianne Moore, alright? But he's doing it with old redhead Kingman, and after five years of getting it whenever, wherever, however she wanted it, full cooperation from the eager young stud, suddenly poor old Hot Damn is supposed to go cold turkey?"

"Excuse me," Danielle said. "Can I say something?"

"Hey, girl," Shawna said, "Why do you say 'excuse me' every time? You got the right to say whatever you want!"

"Go ahead," Big Joe said. "I'm listening."

"What I want to say is this," Danielle said. "What if your wife one night says no, and you force her anyway? I mean, will you rape her, just because she's slept with you for years before?"

"I get it," he said. "But how do we know that he really said no? It's only what he's claiming, what he testified. And that woman, Kingman, she's tough, it's true, but she could be telling the truth, right? She testified she never pressured him to have sex. It's his word against hers."

They were all silent, digesting what Big Joe said.

Miss Hill broke the silence. "I ask you, these people manage money, lots of money, and they're so careful about every little thing. And they promoted him many times, even to vice president. But then, all of a sudden, because of one mistake—not stealing, not hitting, not cursing—only one innocent mistake with that computer document—and suddenly he's no good anymore?"

"Yeah," Abdul said. "That whole explanation sounded kind of iffy."

"That's what I'm saying." Miss Hill shook her finger. "And if they're lying about that, maybe they're lying about the rest?"

CHAPTER 66

After two days in the ICU and a marked improvement in his condition, Thump was moved to the regular floor for monitoring. His room had an extra cot for Mrs. Jefferson. O'Connor came to visit him in the early evening and found a physical therapist working with him. He was still pale and weak, but his smile was back, perhaps because Tiffany was also there, her uniform indicating that it was either before or after a shift.

O'Connor placed a tray on the side table and removed the aluminum foil, exposing a chocolate cake with white frosting and a message written with sprinkles: *Thump that embolism!*

"How cute!" Mrs. Jefferson clapped. "But that's not your sense of humor, is it?"

"It's Jerald," O'Connor said. "He loves to bake."

The physical therapist left, and Thump patted the bed next to him.

She came over and sat. "How are you feeling?"

"Thumped up." He smiled.

O'Connor took his hand. "You're strong. You'll be fine."

"Yup." He looked down at his hand, which she was holding. "I feel better already."

"Davis came by yesterday," she said. "They made an offer. Six months' salary plus medical and a basic letter of reference saying that you left in good standing. It's up to you whether or not to accept it."

"What do you recommend?"

"It's a business decision, not legal. I think our chances with the jury stand at fifty-fifty. We might lose. And even if we win, the jury could award a small amount of money. You have to decide. Do you want to bet on the jury or take this modest settlement?"

He looked at her for a moment, then spoke quietly. "I want a verdict." He held his thumb up, then down. "Win. Or lose. I'll take my chances."

O'Connor looked at Mrs. Jefferson and Tiffany, who both nodded in agreement.

"What about you?" Thump's forehead glistened with sweat. "If we lose, you won't make a dime for all your hard work."

"It's fine." O'Connor wiped his forehead with a tissue. "This case was good for me in other ways."

"Still, you have to pay the bills."

"Don't worry." She smiled. "With all this free press, I'll make out like a bandit."

CHAPTER 67

In the jury room, Big Joe and Abdul were sitting at the table across from each other, their hands locked in arm wrestling while the four women watched. The balance tipped in one direction, then the other, while both men trembled and flushed with the effort.

Shawna sipped Coke from a can with a straw, finishing it with loud slurping. "Time's up, boys." She put down the can. "Age and experience against youth and beauty—it's a tie."

The two men let go with loud exhalations.

"Good job!" Lin clapped fast and lightly. "Now we go back to work!"

Everyone settled down in their seats.

Looking at her notes, Lin asked, "What about the injury? Many broken bones? That was very bad."

"The guy was clumsy." Big Joe folded and straightened his arm, flexing his muscles. "He tripped off the sidewalk. How can you blame a company for an accident like that? What's next? Blame KKG for causing thunder and lightning?"

Everyone laughed, and Shawna said, "My ex-husband got hit by lightning. Who said God doesn't hear prayers?"

Miss Hill shook a finger at her.

"But still," Danielle said, "that Kingman woman, she humiliated him, made him beg. It's disgusting!"

"It's written," Big Joe said. "Hell hath no fury like a woman scorned."

"Well put, Professor," Shawna said.

Lin tapped her pen on the table. "Question is about law, about who is responsible. Miss Kingman is not nice, but she didn't push him into the road, right?"

They looked at each other, considering her point.

"I don't know," Danielle said. "Does it have to be physical pushing? She upset him so much, and then she saw that he walked backward, but she didn't warn him."

"She was upset too," Big Joe said. "Maybe she didn't notice he was about to fall? There's no evidence to blame her for his injuries."

"What about the last thing?" Abdul read from a page in the judge's jury instructions, which he had highlighted. "Here's the definition: '*Intentional infliction of emotional distress is extreme and outrageous conduct that caused severe emotional distress.*' Did they prove it?"

"Just listening to all this legal gibberish," Shawna said, "gives me emotional distress."

"It's not so bad," Big Joe said. "Let's make a list of the things that they did to him. Then we'll discuss how bad they were, if any were extreme and outrageous. Then, on a different sheet of paper, let's write down a list of the things that happened to him, like losing his job, his health, his chances with other companies, his fiancée, all that, and discuss how much he really suffered—what did you call it?"

"Uh, wait a minute." Abdul looked at the instructions again. "It needs to be '*severe emotional distress.*' Whatever that means."

"Severe," Miss Hill said. "Adjective—acute, serious, terrible, dreadful."

"It's simple," Big Joe said. "We write down the two lists and see if they're connected, like one thing was the reason for a thing in the other list, and how *acute* it was for him, you know?"

Around the table, everyone nodded.

Lin tore two sheets from her yellow pad and gave one to Big Joe and one to Abdul. "We're ready. Who wants to go first?"

CHAPTER 68

Two days later, in the afternoon, rain pelted the windows as Judge Clarence worked in his chambers. He was interrupted by a knock on the door, and the courtroom deputy entered.

"Your Honor," he said. "The jury has reached a verdict in *Jefferson v. KKG Investment Management Inc.*"

"Thank you," Judge Clarence said. "Notify the attorneys. And let security know to expect a whole bunch of media folks. I don't want a circus in my courtroom."

"Yes, sir." The deputy left.

Judge Clarence returned to what he was working on, but a moment later put down his pen and leaned back in the large executive chair. "What a case," he said. "What a fucking case."

"It's my case," Thump said from the bed while Mrs. Jefferson put down the phone. "I have to be there when they deliver the verdict."

"Thurgood Marshall Jefferson," she said, "I beg you to be reasonable. Your own lawyer, this moment, told me there is no need for you to be there. You are a very sick boy."

"I'm not a boy." Thump struggled to sit up. "I'm a grown man and I'm the plaintiff. I want to look them in the eye."

"May the good Lord be my shepherd!" Mrs. Jefferson looked up in reverence. "Not four days yet out of intensive care, and you want to go out of the hospital, through the rain, to the same crowded courtroom where you collapsed?"

"That's right." Lowering one leg off the bed, Thump realized he had to deal with the tubes coming down from the IV bag on the other side. "Either you help me, or I'll pull out all this plumbing and crawl out of here on my own."

Mrs. Jefferson picked up the phone and punched a few numbers. "Tiffany? You better get down here quick, honey. He's gone mad!"

At the KKG building, Mr. Kolbe, Henrietta Kingman, Arthur Goldberg, and Bo Chang rode down in the elevator together. No one said a word. In the lobby, each pulled an umbrella from an umbrella stand before stepping out into the rain.

They walked down Charles Street, their blue umbrellas open, showing in white letters the name of *KKG*.

At the corner of Lombard Street, the homeless man was sitting under a store canopy. He got up and watched them proceed toward the federal district courthouse. The rain grew heavier yet, and traffic came to a standstill.

CHAPTER 69

It was four in the afternoon by the time the packed courtroom was ready to hear the verdict. The jurors sat tensely in the jury box, aware that everyone's attention was focused on them, searching for clues in their facial expressions as to the outcome of their lengthy deliberations.

At the plaintiff's table, O'Connor sat by Thump, who had an IV pole attached to his wheelchair. A few rows behind, among the audience, Tiffany sat with Mrs. Jefferson, Andy, and Tecumseh.

At the defense table, Davis and his associate, Ms. Dropper, shuffled their papers while Mr. Kolbe, Kingman, Goldberg, and Chang sat in anxious silence.

In the very back, the homeless man stood by the wall, dripping water.

Judge Clarence addressed Lin, who served as jury foreman. "As to Plaintiff's claim that defendant, KKG Investment Management Inc., through its negligence, caused him physical injuries, what's your verdict?"

Lin looked at the paper in her hand. "We find for the defendant."

The four KKG partners broke into smiles. Davis nodded, his face remaining tense. Behind them, audience members murmured, but silence returned immediately.

"Second," Judge Clarence said, "as to Plaintiff's claim of sexual harassment, what's your verdict?"

Lin looked at her notes again. She started to speak, but her voice was choked with nervousness, and she had to clear her throat. "Sorry," she said, glancing at the many faces, all eyes on her. "Yes, with sexual harassment claim, we find for—"

She hesitated.

"—the plaintiff."

"Yes!" Thump banged a fist on the wheelchair armrest. "Yes! Yes! Yes!"

The audience erupted with talking and some clapping.

"Order in the courtroom!" Judge Clarence pounded the gavel. "Order!"

The four KKG partners' faces fell.

"Madam foreman," Judge Clarence said, "have you awarded damages for the cause of action of sexual harassment?"

"Yes," Lin said, again looking at her notes. "We award to the plaintiff damages in the total amount of—"

Again, she hesitated.

"—one dollar."

"What?" Thump turned to O'Connor. "One dollar?"

A collective groan came from the audience, but Davis smiled for the first time, turning to his clients, nodding in satisfaction.

O'Connor placed a calming hand on Thump's forearm and whispered into his ear. "They're sending a message that they disapprove of KKG, that there was sexual harassment, but they also think that you were at fault."

"Me?"

"By creating the sexual atmosphere that surrounded you during your employment."

Judge Clarence pounded his gavel a few times until silence was restored. "And as to the cause of action of intentional infliction of emotional distress, what's your verdict?"

Lin looked at her fellow jurors, who were all looking up at her. "On the cause of action of intentional infliction of emotional distress," she said, glancing again at her notes as if she wasn't sure, "we find for the plaintiff."

This elicited very little response from the audience, still numb from the miniscule award on the sexual harassment cause.

"Thank you," Judge Clarence said. "Have you awarded damages for this claim?"

Lin looked at her notes yet again. "Yes. For the cause of action of intentional infliction of emotional distress we award to the plaintiff compensatory damages in the amount of one-and-a-half million dollars—"

The rest of her words were buried in yelling and cheering.

Now completely confused, Thump again turned to O'Connor, who shrugged, a smile creeping onto her face.

"Order!" Judge Clarence leaned forward and yelled into his microphone. "Be quiet or I'll clear out this courtroom and continue behind closed doors!"

When silence finally returned, Lin continued. "As I said, for the cause of action of intentional infliction of emotional distress, we award to the plaintiff compensatory damages of one-and-a-half million dollars."

"Very well," the judge said. "Have you awarded any punitive damages?"

"Yes," Lin said. "We awarded to the plaintiff punitive damages of an amount equal to the compensatory damages, which is one-and-a-half million dollars, for a total verdict of damages in the amount of three million dollars."

This time the judge didn't try to control the euphoria. He quickly thanked the jury and adjourned the case until next week, reserving all of the parties' rights for postjudgment motions.

The jurors filed out, the judge disappeared behind the bench, and O'Connor bent to hug Thump, whose eyes shed tears of joy.

Tiffany, Mrs. Jefferson, and Jerald came to the front, crossing paths with Mr. Kolbe, Henrietta Kingman, Arthur Goldberg, and Bo Chang, who were leaving, their faces turned away.

Davis and Dropper stopped to shake hands with O'Connor.

"Congratulations, Ruth."

"Thank you."

Davis signaled to Dropper to leave and lowered his voice, leaning closer to O'Connor. "You understand that my clients will not let this verdict stand. We'll appeal it, go all the way to the Supreme Court if necessary, unless your client agrees to settle now. We can discuss the amount, maybe they'll agree to raise it a little—"

"John," she interrupted him, "would you deliver a message to your clients?"

He nodded.

"Here it is." O'Connor stuck out her middle finger.

A few minutes later, when the courtroom was nearly empty, Thump held both of O'Connor's hands. "I owe you everything," he said. "Everything!"

"It's your victory," she said. "And it's too early to celebrate. They're going to appeal. Might take a long time to collect the judgment."

"We've already collected justice," Thump said. "You and me, we thumped them!"

"Yes, we did," O'Connor said, and for the first time since he had met her, she laughed out loud.

Out in the hallway, Mrs. Jefferson pushed Thump's wheelchair while Tiffany walked beside them. He looked up and saw the homeless man standing by the wall.

"Hey, man!" Thump beckoned him over. "Come over here."

He stepped over haltingly.

"This is my mom." Thump pointed. "And this is Tiffany. I'm sorry, but I don't know your name."

The homeless man shrugged. "You can call me Ezekiel."

The two women nodded and smiled.

"How are you?" Thump reached from his chair and pressed the man's hand. "I'm not working there, on Charles Street anymore, you know, since the accident."

Ezekiel nodded, wringing his hands.

"I didn't remember anything, but they told me you were the first to help me out."

Mumbling something, Ezekiel started to move away.

"Thanks for coming here," Thump said. "It's a good day—we got back some of the success."

"God bless." Ezekiel pointed up. "Now he'll give you health."

"That's right!" Thump patted the wheelchair armrests. "Health is next."

"And happiness," Ezekiel said, moving off faster down the hallway. "Happiness also."

"Thank you," Mrs. Jefferson called after him. "May the good Lord be with you!"

Thump looked up at Tiffany. "Happiness?"

She shrugged.

"Tiff," he said, "the past, what happened, I can't change it. But the future, that's ahead, and I am committed. Will you give me a chance?"

"Maybe," she said. "No promises. Or vows."

They smiled at each other, and he took her hand.

Jerald collected the files into a rollaway briefcase, and they left the courtroom. At the door, O'Connor paused and watched as, down the hallway, Mrs. Jefferson was pushing Thump's wheelchair, and he was holding hands with Tiffany.

"Look," O'Connor pointed.

Jerald smiled. "That's the real victory he hired you for."

"You think?" She looked again, and they were no longer holding hands. "I wouldn't call it a victory. The trial may have helped him win back her heart, but winning back her trust will take a long time."

"They have time. They're young."

At the end of the hallway, a group of reporters and a TV cameraman greeted Thump with questions.

O'Connor took Jerald's arm and turned the other way. "Come, there's another elevator."

They took the staff elevator down with two policemen guarding an overweight black man in orange prison garb and shackles. He glanced at O'Connor, and his face lit up.

"Hey, Judgie! How you doin'?"

"Doing real well," O'Connor said. "And you?"

"No complaints." He grinned. "Remember me?"

She shook her head.

"You sent me to Brockbridge six years ago. Second-degree assault."

"Are you still there?"

"No way. I was out in eight months."

"But you're back in?"

"It's all a big misunderstandin', you know?" He rattled his shackles. "Hey, word on the street is you switched sides."

"Excuse me?"

"You helpin' a brother, ain't you?" He held his cuffed hands together, rubbing forefingers. "You and us, workin' together against the system."

Jerald laughed, and one of the officers pushed down on the prisoner's hands.

The elevator slowed down to a stop.

"Best of luck to you," O'Connor said. "Stay out of trouble."

"You too, Judgie. You too." At the officers' prodding, he obediently stepped closer to the doors. "How about a business card?"

She slipped her card into the breast pocket of his shirt.

"Appreciate it! I'll call you—"

The doors opened and the officers shoved him out.

"Hey," he yelled over his shoulder, "will you take my call?"

O'Connor glanced at Jerald before answering. "Yes," she said. "I'll be happy to."

The End

ACKNOWLEDGEMENTS

As with my other novels, the factual details underlying the story required research and verification. In achieving this level of authenticity, I have benefited invaluably from the works of many scholars and authors.

Especially helpful were Erwin Chemerinsky's *Constitutional Law* (Aspen, 2009), Catherine MacKinnon and Reva Siegel's *Directions in Sexual Harassment Law* (Yale, 2012), Samuel Estreicher and Michael C. Harper's *Cases and Materials on Employment Discrimination Law* (West, 2012), and the decisions of the US Supreme Court in *Meritor v. Vinson* (1986), *Harris v. Forklift* (1993), *Faragher v. Boca* (1998), *Burlington Industries v. Ellerth* (1998), and *Oncale v. Sundowner* (1998). Without the incredible courage and resilience of the plaintiffs in these (and many other) cases, victims of workplace sexual harassment would not have the legal protections now available to them.

I owe a great debt of gratitude to Stephen J. Wall, who has read every first draft of every one of my novels (and more than a few subsequent drafts) and never failed to tell me the truth, the whole truth, and nothing but the truth. Thank you, Steve!

For reading various drafts of this novel, I am grateful to Steve Kelly, Carol Wilner, Don Eddins, Janice Petrovich, Fiona Meller Azrieli, Talya Azrieli, Sarai Azrieli, Hanan Gur, Kevin Carlson, Lisa Klein Schneiderman, Sivan Chaban, Sharon Glazer, and Tamas Karpati, who provided thoughtful observations, critical comments, and enthusiastic encouragement. Similarly, thanks to Lyn Vaus and the workshop participants at the Bethesda Writer Center for their helpful input during my work on the screenplay version of this story.

Proofreading was provided by Jesse Rafe Meyerson and Janelle Logan. Editing and design were provided by editor Renee Johnson and the team at CreateSpace, who together made this novel a success.

And last but not least, to my readers, whose enjoyment is the purpose of my work. As always, your comments and thoughts are greatly appreciated. An e-mail contact is provided through the website at: www.AzrieliBooks.com

ALSO BY AVRAHAM AZRIELI

Fiction:

The Masada Complex – A Novel
The Jerusalem Inception – A Novel
The Jerusalem Assassin – A Novel
Christmas for Joshua – A Novel
The Mormon Candidate – A Novel

Nonfiction:

Your Lawyer on a Short Leash
One Step Ahead – A Mother of Seven Escaping Hitler

AUTHOR'S WEBSITE:

www.AzrieliBooks.com

Made in the USA
Charleston, SC
22 February 2014